THE DISTANCE BETWEEN

THE DISTANCE BETWEEN

Eliza Osborne

Copyright © 2000 by Eliza Osborne

Published by
Soho Press, Inc.
853 Broadway
New York, N.Y. 10003

Library of Congress Cataloging-in-Publication Data

Osborne, Eliza, 1946–
    The distance between / Eliza Osborne.
        p.   cm.
    ISBN 1-56947-180-0   (alk. paper)
    I. Title.
    PS3565.S427057   2000   99-30694
    813'.54—dc21   CIP

10 9 8 7 6 5 4 3 2 1

In loving memory of my father

THE DISTANCE BETWEEN

CHAPTER ONE

IF THE HITCHHIKER hadn't looked so very pregnant, Mattie would never have slowed the car. Even when she had time, Mattie didn't pick up strangers, no matter how guilt-ridden their hunched shoulders or their February sneakers or their feigned indifference made her feel. But to drive past a woman in this stage of pregnancy was probably an actionable offense. A farmer crunching corn stalks in a nearby field would take your license number, have you up on charges of neglect, and some mother-weighted jury would award the unborn child four and a quarter million dollars in damages, and the mother-to-be more than that, for pain and suffering. Besides, Mattie's children were young enough for her to remember all that was involved in moving your pregnant self, all in one piece, from one location to another.

Mattie pulled to a stop on the shoulder of the road, then backed up slowly, carefully, as though the lumpy spot that was a woman in her rearview mirror might suddenly sprint forward, falling under Mattie's wheels. Pregnant women always made Mattie act in careful ways. Mattie had been sixteen and learning to drive by the time her mother got around to her last pregnancy, and Mattie could remember driving the whole family down a deserted country road one Sunday afternoon, her orange learner's permit flapping on the dashboard. Going twenty-five serious miles per hour, Mattie had driven in a straight line up a long incline, cresting she was sure the highest hill in Pennsylvania. Then Mattie had put the car in park and turned off the ignition. She was not about to risk her pregnant mother to the steep descent. And so, had Mattie's mother survived the ride that Sunday afternoon, only to die in another car crash on another day? This day. No, of course not.

Mattie got out and waved to the young woman, who stood fixed in place. "Hello," Mattie said. The warm whish of a passing tractor trailer truck lifted Mattie's skirt.

"Hi." Mattie walked closer. "You need a ride?"

The woman nodded.

"Are you okay?"

"What do you think?" The pregnant woman rubbed her pudgy fingers back and forth across her nose.

Good deeds in real life were never like the Girl Scouts led you to believe.

"Where are you heading?" Mattie said.

"Wherever."

"Okay. Well, I can give you a lift, but I'm in a rush. I'm on my way to Pennsylvania."

"This is Pennsylvania."

"Oh, right," Mattie said, "I was thinking I was still in New York. It all looks pretty much the same."

The woman lumbered over to the car and slid her body into the front seat, fat but agile.

"The seat belt's by your shoulder," Mattie said.

The young woman sighed, a hot sigh for this late in November, and they drove off in silence. It's amazing, Mattie thought, how quickly any twosome set up the working elements of their brand-new relationship. Within the first five minutes, major ground rules are in operation, and you have each nestled into the position you are very likely to maintain.

The air enclosure surrounding this pregnant woman gave Mattie a pretty clear idea of about how many questions she was likely interested in being asked. Mattie worked on phrasing two or three that never reached a form that sounded off-the-cuff enough. So when's your baby due? revised from, When was your baby due? What are you doing on the highway? which after several miles turned into, How old are you? And, Are you married? which became, Are you quite safe out here all alone and should you be walking any distance? But Mattie wasn't even comfortable with, What's your name? She squirmed in her seat, felt self-conscious, definitely ill at ease. "It is my car." Mattie wasn't sure whether she had spoken the words out loud, but her passenger gave no sign, seemed intent on studying the horizon. Mattie checked her watch: 12:15. She had been on the road since nine. Five more hours. Six, tops.

But to reach what circumstance, what relief or what calamity, Mattie had no clue. She ought to be formulating possibilities right now, conjuring the full array of injuries that might follow in the wake of any crash.

"We had this stupid reunion."

"I beg your pardon?" Mattie turned toward the lumpy profile.

"A reunion."

"A reunion," Mattie said.

"That's how come I'm out here hitching. I didn't want to go in the first place, and then four hundred fat, nosy relatives were all stuffing their faces and talking about me behind my back. So I just took off. It was too hot there anyway."

"So that's why you were hitchhiking."

"No. That's not why I was hitchhiking. I mean, what do you think I am, some kind of jerk, or what? I was hitchhiking because of my mother. Those old cows were trying every trick in the book to get me to say who little Bozo's daddy was, or is to be, and I told this whole pile of aunts and stupid cousins it was none of their beeswax, and told my mother to give me the keys, and she said no. It's her fault I'm pregnant in the first place."

"Your mother's fault," Mattie said.

"What is there, an echo in this car, or what?"

"Where would you like me to drop you?"

"Oh, right here would be dandy. I'm very good at figuring out where I'm not welcome."

"Look," Mattie said, "I'll take you where you'd like to go."

"I'd like to go to New Mexico. The desert. That's where I'd like to go."

"What's your second choice?" Mattie said.

"Ugh, ughh! Oh my God!"

Mattie swerved the wheel.

"What?" Mattie said. "What's wrong?"

"Ughh! I just got this pain in my back and down into my legs. Ughh! Oh my God! I think it's the baby."

Conversation had been difficult enough with this woman. Mattie had no inclination to be the whole of the welcoming committee for her offspring.

"Where's the hospital?" Mattie said.

"I think I'm okay now. It's passed."

"It doesn't work that way. Where's the hospital?"

"Back the other way."

Mattie put her four-way flasher on, a reflex in any crisis: if it started to rain, or one of the kids said he thought he was going to throw up, if the car made a funny metal clanking sound, if a stranger threatened to give birth in the front seat. Mattie saw a cut across the median, which was more of a gully than she would have navigated if she had felt there was a choice. At the low point came another scream.

"Oh my God! My God! Oh!"

"Breathe," Mattie said. "Did you take classes for Lamaze? Breathe. Pant like a dog."

It was the only breathing exercise Mattie could remember, and she was fairly sure it was for fast contractions in Stage 4, but Mattie felt that using breathing techniques for labor was a lot like taking aspirin for a brain tumor or hot tea for toxic shock: it created the illusion you were doing something, when anyone who had been through Stage 1 of labor could tell you morphine and/or unconsciousness were the only ideas that made any sense.

"Oh. It's gone. My God."

Mattie narrowly avoided being hit, pulling into the fast-moving traffic. "Now, where's the hospital?" Mattie said.

"Get off, the first exit. Go right. Will you call my mother?"

"I'll call anyone you want. Let's just get you taken care of."

Traffic was at a standstill up ahead, and Mattie took the shoulder of the road before anyone else got the idea first.

∽

"How are you doing?" Mattie peeked around a wall of white sheet hanging on a rod. She would just say good-bye and good luck to her pregnant rider, who had told the admitting nurse her name was Sherry Hicks, and Mattie would be on her way. She hadn't lost ten minutes.

"I hate this place," Sherry said. "I hate all hospitals."

"Yeah, well, trust me on this one," Mattie said. "There's no place like it when you're in labor."

"Where's my mother?"

"Well, we can't exactly reach her, but we left a message. Are you sure there's no one else to call?"

"I want my mother." Sherry tried to roll over and sit up, but the next spasm tacked her down.

"The nurses said they will keep trying. She will be here any minute. How's it going?"

"It's hell. That's how it's going."

"Well, it'll be over before you know it," Mattie said, "and you'll have the sweetest little baby in your arms, and you won't even remember that it hurt."

"That's bullshit," Sherry said. "I don't want a sweet little baby. I want to get the hell out of here. I want to live in New Mexico on a ranch in the desert in..."

The particulars of the American Southwest were lost to the next contraction. Mattie turned to run out for the nurse.

"Don't leave me!" A stuck-pig squeal.

"I'll get someone to help."

"Don't go," Sherry said.

"Okay. Okay. I'm here. Just try to relax. Look at that fire extinguisher. Look at it. Bore a hole in it with your eyes. Look at it so hard you make the baking soda gush out through the cracks every time you have a contraction. It's called a focal point. Has it eased up? Let yourself go limp. That gets you ready for the next one."

"You go fuck yourself."

"You know, I wish I could stay until your mother comes, but I really have to be on my way. I wish I could stay."

"Yeah, sure you do. I bet you would just love to hang around and get to hold little Martin."

"Oh, Martin," Mattie said.

"Martin. John. Paul. Harry. Fred. What the hell do I care. Tell you what, stick around and I'll let you name the baby. Better yet, I'll give you the baby, free. No, for ten thousand cash. I'll give you the baby for five thousand. Be a sport."

"Let me get a nurse," Mattie said. "She'll be much more helpful."

Mattie left in a hurry before the next wave of pain, or venom, had a chance to crest and break.

"I heard my girl, Sherry, was here." Mattie saw a skinny, badly weathered woman, leaning on the counter of the nurses' station. She was not a hitchhiker Mattie would pick up, not even pregnant.

The nurse did not look up, did not cease repeating her blunt-needle jabs into the doughy hand of a woman who looked far beyond the other side of caring.

"Can you hear me? I'm here to see my girl. I got dragged off in the middle of a family reunion that was just getting off the ground." This last directed to the curling Formica counter covering, and to Mattie, as much as to the oblivious nurse.

"I think I might be able to help you," Mattie said.

"In just what way is that?" the woman bristled, that is, her hair seemed to stick out stiffer, straighter.

"Your daughter, I believe, is down the corridor, the last room on the left."

"You people. Why didn't you say so in the first place. Leave me standing here whistling in the wind. You're all alike."

Mattie stopped to consider. She ought to say her last good-bye to Sherry, but the mother and daughter should have their moment first. The nurse was taping on the IV needle, and the woman slouching in the chair sat with her mouth drooping, drooling, or relaxed enough to drool. Mattie could remember in Lamaze class being taught to drool, a warm-up for indignities that no one thought to mention in advance, knowing, if they once considered it, that given the proper dose of pain you will lose sensitivities that were several solemn generations in the making.

"Sherry Hicks." The nurse addressing Mattie stared at a spot over Mattie's shoulder. "We have her OB chart here. You realize the pelvis is a good three-quarters of a centimeter under size. We'll let her start, but you can figure on a section." The word made Mattie even more glad of hospitals and doctors and nurses and delivery rooms that were open seven days a week. "The last ultrasound measured fetal weight in excess of nine pounds." The nurse raised her gaze and scowled at Mattie as though she were in no small measure responsible for the baby's size. "Nine pounds, fourteen ounces, and that was just before Halloween." The implication seemed to be, the unborn child might have been out trick-or-treating in the interim.

"I'm not a relative," Mattie said. "Actually, I'm in a hurry."

"A hurry. Are you her coach?"

"Her coach?" Mattie imagined herself gyrating on the sidelines of a brightly lighted court where twenty or thirty seven-foot-tall bodies hurtled past, and back again, pursuing basketballs, inside a noisy and sweat-crowded gym.

"Her labor coach." The nurse managed six syllables where four had always been.

"Oh," Mattie said. She had forgotten. Perhaps purposely. Mattie hated all the jargon borrowed willy-nilly for whatever enterprise, where words and phrases were appropriated, stolen, misapplied. You could not embark on any activity without learning a newly minted language or an altered application for the one you already knew.

"No, I'm not her coach."

"A friend?"

"I don't even know her," Mattie said. "I picked her up out on the highway and brought her here."

"Well, I hardly think it is appropriate, under the circumstances, for you to involve yourself at this level in her medical care."

"Exactly," Mattie said. "I'll just say good-bye then."

"Well, please don't agitate her. She's a primapara."

Mattie walked off.

Primapara.

Prima donna.

The corridor was silent, comatose between contractions.

Mattie rapped almost soundlessly on the door and walked into the tiny labor room.

"Oops. Wrong room," Mattie started to say, then stopped herself.

She saw a fat stranger lying dead across the bed, or she looked dead.

"Ice." A message from the other side.

Mattie scrinched her mouth up into something very small and wrinkled, standing still as death herself.

"Ice." The woman on the bed began to breathe again, the way a mountain might breathe if something had just made the mountain angry. And the woman kept on breathing. It was like good theater, when you forget yourself for half a minute and just watch. There was nothing in the room but one breath, and only when it left, another. Then the woman seemed to fall asleep, went back to looking dead.

"Ice," she said.

"Ice," Mattie said.

"I need more ice." It seemed such a consolidated and well-ordered wish.

"Right," Mattie said.

She wondered if the woman were blind, if she would never see her child's sweet face.

Mattie took the small container dripping on the table beside the bed, and headed out to find the nurse. She needed to get out of here. But halfway down the corridor she saw a kitchen, walked in, feeling very medical, and opened up the freezer. Right the first time. There was a huge bag of chipped ice. Mattie filled her pink bucket to the top. She loved to have a lot of anything. Then she walked back to the room. The mountain was up to its old tricks. Mattie was almost sure the woman was exhaling more air than she took in. Mattie put the ice down. The woman still hadn't opened her eyes.

"Thank you." It sounded like good-bye.

"Can I get you anything else?" Mattie said.

But the woman was gone, off to sleep again.

Mattie looked around the dusky room as though something in need of doing might be apparent there. But it seemed like a room where everything had been attended to, a room that didn't need a thing.

"Can I get you anything else?" Mattie did not whisper.

No reply.

"So." Louder. "If there is nothing else then."

A woman who would not be summoned back. Having a baby is like dying. It requires your full attention. It demands it. Absorbing all of you, putting all your other plans on hold. No matter what.

The woman lying there had not even seen Mattie's face, and in a week, or in four hours' time, Mattie wouldn't remember hers either. Mattie would be gone before the child was born. Lives touch that way. Ping. Smash. Graze. Collide. Then veer off again without exchanging any small memento. Mattie never would run into little Joe or Henrietta on the street, would never say, I gave your mother ice when she was having you, when she was so all by herself, the day before she was your mother.

Mattie's mother had been all alone, when she was having Mattie. They had sent her husband home, told him there was no need for him to lose a night's sleep, babies were born every day. And so for the thirty-seven hours that would be her labor, she was all by herself.

And what if Mattie had knocked on that wrong door, in that long ago September, what if Mattie had been there, all starched in white, brisk and efficient. What if Mattie had stood there beside her mother's bed, her long, cool fingers schooled in telling progress in small numbered centimeters, wringing water from a flannel cloth a hundred times to cool her mother's brow, feeding bucketsful of ice in slivers, at intervals spaced wide enough to make the wish for ice a thing substantial and sustaining. Mattie might have timed contractions to the fraction of a second, might have said, "You're doing fine. Just fine. She's coming. I can see the head. A baby girl. A healthy baby girl, who will grow up straight and tall, with curly auburn hair, a fine girl who will run faster than the wind, and play the violin, and think her life a matter of some pleasure." (It was not unthinkable the baby born that day might, but for the auburn hair, have had certain thoughts of turning out in just that way.)

But Mattie's role that day had been something else entirely. She was not cast as the nurse. She did not even have a speaking part. Maybe it explained the years that followed. Maybe Mattie and her mother just got off on the wrong foot.

A choir of women started up on some obstetric cue. First one lead soloist, then two or three other, hoarser voices joining in, like when one baby in the nursery cries, awakening the others. Nurses in colored smocks moved in and out of rooms, crossing back and forth and back again, doing a job Mattie would never do, not in this or any other lifetime.

By tomorrow, or the next day at the very latest, Mattie thought, every one of these vocal women will be mothers. The nurses here will teach them how to bathe and shampoo their newborns, how to dust their lungs with baby powder, (as though cleanliness were godliness and not just a neighbor). They'll teach them how to use a breast pump, and tell them which end of the bottle to hold, and how to change a diaper. Then they'll put the two new relatives in a wheelchair together and push them out the door, all tucked up in baby blankets and warm wishes, waffling hormones and bewilderment.

It's like giving a brain surgeon six minutes on the basics:

Here's the brain. This is right. This is left. Sharp outcuts dull. Too little is better than too much. Always wear fresh gloves. Then a handshake and a hearty slap on the back, and the rest is on-the-job training.

Mattie knocked on Sherry's open door.

"Give me that blanket. I'm freezing my ass off."

Mattie walked in on motherhood present, eyeball to eyeball, with the ghost of motherhood-to-be.

"Don't get your bowels in an uproar." Sherry's mother moved like a slow boat in the water, a barge, moving against the current. She covered her daughter only to see the blanket slip beneath her with the next heave.

"Hold my hand." The words were fashioned out of metal. "Don't let go."

Mattie focused on the two clutched hands, one fat and pink and puffy, one gnarled, a map in bas relief with liver spots for lakes and long blue veins to mark land elevations. Mattie watched the hands, tried to see the current, the connection that allowed the sallow woman to sustain the whale beached on the far-too-narrow bed. (The books said the birthing mother may take comfort in lying with her partner during labor. A suggestion suited to the ninety-nine-pound pregnant gymnast.) Sherry's body took on some new shape. Her several parts shifted and she lay back in something like composure, studying a spot that wasn't there, on the ceiling overhead. All of this seemed to cost Sherry's mother nothing, diminishing her not at all. She gave to Sherry and she didn't lose. She helped her daughter. It was obvious. But at no cost to herself. You don't need to bleed yourself to do a pretty tidy tourniquet. And this, all of it, was novel in Mattie's experience. With her own mother, every touch cost something.

"Excuse me," Mattie said. "I just wanted to say good-bye and good luck."

"Oh yeah." Sherry went back to her perusal of the ceiling, having lost her spot.

"Is that all you have to say, young lady?" Sherry's mother grew an inch.

"Oh yeah, thanks a bunch." She spoke as though by providing transportation it was Mattie who had put her in this fix.

"She always did choke on her please and thank-yous, but she thanks her lucky stars it was you and not some sex-crazed maniac who picked her up out there."

Mattie tried not to visualize the oversize Sherry in the maniac's Corvette.

"Yeah, right." Sherry made it sound almost conversational. "They got any TV here?"

Mattie shrugged. What show would you want to watch during labor? *Let's Make a Deal. The Edge of Night. All My Children. Wall Street Week.* Certainly nothing with Barbara Walters.

"You wanna ask the nurse?" Sherry's mother half-turned to Mattie. The hand that held Sherry's looked a deeper pink but no less connected.

"Well, okay. But then I have to be on my way. My parents were in a car wreck this morning." Mattie would have said "accident," not "wreck," if she were still in New York State. "I'm going to see them. To see that they're okay. I still have another five hours' drive." This seemed so strange to say. Mattie was not entirely sure she wasn't making the whole thing up.

"What's the matter? You never heard of telephones?" Sherry started to change position, then seemed to think better of the idea.

"No," Mattie said, "it was a bad accident. I want to be there."

"I mean telephones along the way," Sherry said, "like pay phones, like the phones they have in maternity wards to call and say 'Little Junior just popped out' could be used to call another hospital to see if someone's parents were okay."

Mattie did not want to call, had not wanted to until she got there. She did not want to drive in the same car with any news.

"I think I'd better just go," Mattie said.

"Suit yourself," Sherry said, "but would you just mention to the ugly nurse there on the way out that some people might like to watch a little TV."

And with the last two letters spoken, Sherry's entire body contracted to half of its original size, and most of that became her vocal cords. Mattie waved to Sherry's mother, who was no longer looking Mattie's way. It was six o'clock that night, and Mattie was in Harrisburg before she thought about the television set again.

CHAPTER TWO

MATTIE PICKED UP speed to pass a station wagon with an empty boat trailer in tow. How much time had she lost with Sherry Hicks? Half an hour at the most. To maybe save a life, a new life. Sometimes it took longer than that to get a burger and fries. It felt like she had been in the maternity ward for hours, for long uninterrupted days. The tricks of time, the sleight of hand of certain minutes, on peculiar days.

By now they were probably wheeling Sherry to the delivery room, with Sherry's skinny mother running to keep up, Sherry hanging on to her for dear life. Birth was so amazing, such a strange, unlikely way to come to be. Mattie had loved giving birth, had reveled in the oddities of pregnancy, the frank, outrageous, sexy fatness of the thing. From eighteen months of living in that altered state, Mattie could bring back only one tense episode, and that occasioned by her mother.

By the time Mattie was pregnant with her first child, she was all but out of touch with her mother. There would be the odd phone call from time to time with news of an uncle's colon cancer or a great aunt's long-anticipated, swift demise, and once, word that lightning had struck Mattie's old bedroom, causing a noisy, short-lived fire. (Mattie's parents would dine out on that blaze for years.) But otherwise, there was no contact.

As her pregnancy progressed, Mattie sometimes had inklings that this impending birth might offer up the makings of some new, long-overdue connection with her mother, give the two of them a common occupation they could fashion into neutral, even sympathetic, conversation. So Mattie would call her mother, with updates on her weight gain (the numbers *were* impressive), and with major revisions of her due date, which was finally fixed at March 16. Thus it would be on the Ides of March that her sister Nancy telephoned at eleven o'clock at night.

"Mum and Dad are coming up in the morning." Nancy had rationed out the words like they were, each of them, expensive.

"Up where?" Mattie had asked in that hormone-husky voice she liked to think made her sound just like Lauren Bacall.

"Up to your place," Nancy had said. "They're bringing a whole ham, even though they know very well Paul's Jewish."

"What are you talking about?"

"They're leaving here at six A.M. to beat the Scranton traffic. They want it to be a surprise, but I felt you would want to know."

"My due date is tomorrow. They haven't been here in four years. I could give birth at any moment."

"That's why they're coming. That's why the ham. And Mum made scalloped potatoes and baked beans and chocolate cake."

"They can't do this to me."

"Well, if you don't want your own parents, you'll have to tell them that yourself." Nancy's tone gave every indication of her having gotten her full money's worth from Ma Bell.

So on the eve of what Mattie had hoped would be the birthday of her longed-for son, on the eve of what turned out to be only a ninety-seven-hour, guilt-infested, but otherwise boring day, Mattie had called her mother, close to midnight, had awakened her in fact, to say, "Give the scalloped potatoes and the cake to the Salvation Army. Eat the ham. Make sandwiches. Have a mid-March picnic, only please don't come to see me. Your last two visits—spaced at four-year intervals—were each memorable miseries, uniquely and distinctly awful for everybody there, yourself included. Don't be offended. Please. I don't ask you to understand. It's pretty late in the proceedings for that. But please, I beg you, stay where you are. We'll call you with the news, first thing."

The guilt attendant on the phone call Mattie made that night occupied her waking hours until April Fool's Day, when Andrew finally appeared, a fortnight late, or maybe right on time.

Mattie had padded her request that night with soft excuses all around. She said she had a sore throat that might be contagious and that the furnace had been on the blink and so the house was cold (not too cold for a newborn, but murder for a couple in their sixties.) She said the doctor told her she would probably be late and they would feel so bad if they came all that way and never got to see the baby. She may have even added that a storm was on its way, and a new strain of flu was infecting the whole neighborhood. No matter. The damage had been neatly done, Mattie's mother feeling wounded and rejected, even more than she felt martyred, and Mattie carrying the guilt of that whole salty ham around with her for years.

It was the stuff and substance of all dealings with her mother. Mattie's mother started it: hardly ever calling or visiting, and when she did, scalding the house and all surrounding with anger and disapproval, and then getting her feelings grandly hurt when someone finally called her on it, and, in the end, devising a surprise attack on Mattie's due date, albeit with a picnic basket and a baby gift, and even, perhaps, fine intentions, (who could tell?) and Mattie to protect her pregnant self, saying no, don't come.

And guess who gets to be the bad guy? The ungrateful, cold, distant daughter, the unloving one? It was always the same. Mattie and her mother's sins and failings getting tangled up together like a dozen balls of string, so that in the end you could never say what was the provocation, what the response, who started it, whose fault it was, who suffered harm the most.

And every crime must have an owner, every happening at least one guilty party, every sin be down to somebody's account. Even acts of God were someone's fault. And there was no statute of limitations on responsibility, so that "Who broke that vase?" might easily become "Who's idea was it to have children in the first place?" And Mattie's mother echoed Freud, "There's no such thing as an accident."

There is no better way to teach guilt to a child.

Mattie's mother stories would refuse to tell at all well to anybody else. "You won't believe what my mother did to me." Mattie to a friend. "She tried to come to visit me and bring me food and help me with the baby."

"Oh, no. How awful. How terrible for you."

Andrew had been eight months old before Mattie's parents had come up "to see the new baby," and sister Nancy, sister spite, would report with some sincere satisfaction, a full year after that, asking Mattie's mother would she be going up to see Andrew in the summer, only to hear her tart reply, "I already saw him."

Mattie could never quite work out just where to put her father in these scenes, what culpability she should assign to him. He told Mattie over and again how deeply he regretted not coming to her wedding.

When Mattie had called her mother to say that she and Paul were getting married, the silence following the announcement was three minutes by the kitchen clock, then finally broken by the plaintive phrase, "I never got over your divorce. We all loved Carlton so very much."

Mattie's mother had hated Carlton. She had treated him with rarefied disdain. There hadn't been the faintest hint of his impending sainthood until the legal separation was official.

"I don't know how I could ever accept another son-in-law in Carlton's place," had been the halting words on the telephone. "If I came to your wedding, I would probably only be able to stand in a corner and cry."

"Then you might be happier not to come." Mattie's words had been squeezed out between migraine pulsations. "I mean probably everybody there is going to be feeling pretty happy for us." (Mattie hadn't known at the time that a week later Paul's mother would be disowning him for being married by an Episcopalian priest and not a rabbi. It didn't matter. Your own mother's performance is always more riveting than anybody else's. Besides, Paul's mother had reclaimed ownership of her son two days before the wedding and had come, albeit dressed in black.)

Mattie's parents had skipped the nuptials, resurrecting the old questions of who's sinned against? who sinned? They missed the whole affair, the champagne, the string quartet, the flowers crowding every corner of the white gazebo on the hill, so unlike Mattie's first, home church wedding where her parents sat with two hundred prim Wesleyan Methodists and eight Episcopalians—from the groom's side—nibbling regulation white cake, drinking fruit punch in the basement of the red-brick church. At that wedding Carlton's Anglican proclivities had been as foreign and no less alarming than Paul's Jewishness would be seven years later, by which time Mattie was herself Episcopalian; although lately she had begun to wonder whether anyone ever really got over his original religion.

"I feel so bad we missed your wedding," Mattie's father said over and again, and Mattie knew he did feel sad. But he could have come. He used to drive all over the place, sometimes taking off for two or three days at a time, calling home to say, "I took a notion to visit Bill and Janet. I'll be back by Sunday night." He could have come alone, he could have weathered whatever dark displeasure he would surely have come home to. He could have come, the man that he was then.

Now he was so different. He sat in the big recliner in the TV room and napped, or went for long walks by himself. He had retired. From life. He seemed deflated, just as surely as if somebody pulled the plug, letting all the air escape. And Mattie could recall when he was bigger than life. She could remember days when he was her salvation.

Mattie's mother had never mentioned the wedding, had made not one passing reference in fifteen years.

Mattie blinked hard twice before she realized that the flickering light was coming from a police cruiser traveling right behind her. It took another several blinks to figure out the lights were flickering for her.

Mattie thought she should by rights have had her license lifted long before she hit the Pennsylvania border. As it was, she stuffed the Pennsylvania speeding ticket behind the visor with the one from Connecticut and the one from New York, adjusted the rearview mirror like she was just starting out, and nodded to the state trooper, who had clocked her going seventy, as though the two of them had come to some agreement that was pleasing to them both. She drove off with exaggerated care.

So much for the computer age, Mattie thought, as she watched the police cruiser shrink and disappear into the rearview mirror. She had been traveling fifty-six miles over the speed limit, if anybody cared to tally the three tickets. But they don't tally them. They write the numbers in their regulation black, slash script, speak them into metal static senders, and they're gone, just like the postcards Mattie never dropped into the mail slots between elevators on the top floors of big hotels, the mail slots she was positive went nowhere. You dropped your letter in and it was no more.

Mattie crept along at fifty-five, the highway open wide for miles ahead, not another car in sight. She passed a roadside rest stop. Four tractor trailer trucks and two small silver-colored cars. Maybe they knew something. Maybe the road ended up ahead. Mattie lifted her foot and let the red indicator drift to the left. Sixty. Fifty-seven. Fifty-four.

She had been lucky. Any one of these state troopers could become unpleasant, these troopers who, Mattie thought, must surely have been born wearing sunglasses and aftershave, these troopers whose gray twill uniforms constrained their bodies always the same way, the shirt fronts tight, pulled taut, straining to hold something in. What? Anger. Maybe violence. Mattie did not want to meet another trooper, did not want to field another minute of regulation politeness. How did these men speak to their wives? Did they have spare voices, alternate vocabularies? Did their uniforms come off?

Mattie thought she should have waited for Paul and the boys. They should all have made the trip together. When the call had come this morning about the accident, Mattie had called the airport and been told there were no flights until the evening. Then she had responded in the way her father would have done: to act first, then consider. Swift, well-intentioned help, always off the mark. Mattie calling out, a child frightened in the night; her father dashing up the stairs, catching threads of a new jacket on a nail, making a clean slit. He had come running, always empty-handed, needing. Not just unequal to the moment, he would respond, exuding all that Mattie knew of love, but still needy himself. Take care of me, his helping said.

A straggly-looking fellow stood, his thumb out, just beyond the Port Justin exit ramp. Mattie kept her eyes trained straight ahead. "Sorry. I already gave." Mattie's father would have picked him up. "Get in," he would growl in a pretended menace. "I'm not afraid to ride with you, if you're not afraid to ride with me." He who feared more things than Mattie could name or remember. He always picked up hitchhikers. In the fifties, Mattie's mother sat through Sunday drives, straddling the hump, sandwiched in between her husband and a stranger, some sailor, or a man who was far from home, a man whose story Mattie's father always got him to recite with all the names of characters and places. Mattie with her brothers and her sister, riding restless in the backseat of one or another black or dark green, musty Buick; in a backseat large enough to hold a dozen thin-limbed children, sitting in a row, their feet stretched straight out, still not touching the front seat.

Buicks. They were always Buicks. One Sunday driving home from church in a new Buick, secondhand, but new to them, Mattie rolled the window down, stuck her head out, shouting, "Super Dynaflo," at no one, and her father yelled at her. Super Dynaflo. Words etched in place with strange embarrassment. In Mattie's mind, words bearing witness to the puzzlement, the curious knowing that some words were bad (you never could anticipate which ones) and that no words ever should be shouted out of windows.

The traffic thickened with the signs for Scranton. How was it all these people had set off in the middle of the day to go to Scranton? Mattie looked at the faces of the drivers in the cars she passed. They looked so purposeful, each heading to one place in particular, a place where they were expected, or a place where their showing up would come as a surprise. How many people were in for a surprise this afternoon in Scranton, Pennsylvania? Maybe thirty, Mattie thought. Fifty at the outside. People don't get surprised all that often. Not really. Except perhaps by news of accidents, and sometimes not even then.

"Mum and Dad were in an accident out on Chestnut Street, in the car," Nancy had said that morning when she called. "I thought you ought to know. We don't really know much yet, but I should tell you, they say it doesn't look too good. You will need to decide for yourself what you should do."

Mattie paid attention to her driving. Through Scranton and Wilkes Barre traffic was heavy.

"Now watch for Eighty-one South to Route Eighty," Mattie said out loud in a tone of voice her sister, Nancy, would have called aggressive, not assertive. Assertive was good. Nancy went to three-day workshops in the Catskills with famous family therapists to learn to be assertive.

"I know you won't like hearing this," Nancy had written in the last communication of any substance that had passed between the sisters, in the letter Mattie had gotten up at 3 A.M. to tear to little pieces, shred to parts of sentences, to single words, almost harmless in themselves. It was a letter, read one time hastily, then once more slowly to make sure, that Mattie could recite verbatim.

"I know you won't like hearing this," Nancy had written, "but you are an aggressive person. When you were in therapy, you changed. You are aggressive, not assertive. I know you must have friends, because you say you see people, but they must be people who can take you. I write this very thoughtfully, and believe me when I say I do not want to hurt you, Mattie, and I just know that you will take offense at this, but you are someone who must have everything her own way, and you don't stop until you get it. You are an aggressive person.

"You ask me in your letter why I have not invited you to stay with us when you've come to town over the past eleven years. It is because I need to be able to get away from you, to go home whenever I can't take you anymore. And I should tell you that I am not the only one who sees you in this way."

Mattie turned on the radio, pushed all five buttons, switched to AM, made a full pass left to right and back again, turned it off, and opened her window a crack. Fresh air. A myth.

There was nothing on this stretch of road, no clues to tell you where you were, or even when. This might be 1971, this road the barren stretch from Rochester to Buffalo, and Mattie might be driving with her first husband, Carlton, in a Ford Mustang, deep maroon, driving through a marriage that did not seem a wasteland at the time. It had seemed, rather, like a long, attenuated Saturday, spent safe and dry, if idly, inside, listening to the rain on the tin roof in the spare bedroom on Nonotuck Street, the whole of one long Saturday spent indoors, the weather outside wet and gray, inside, a yellow light.

Or Mattie might be younger, eight or ten, and traveling on this stretch of highway, riding on a bus beside her grandmother, holding on her lap a cardboard box of white bread, chicken salad sandwiches with all the crusts cut off, and peanut butter cookies, and one orange, to share; on a bus, heading for Youngstown, Ohio, to visit Aunt Ellen, who all the family said had been the ugliest baby ever born, Ellen, who had grown up to resemble no one so much as Marilyn Monroe.

Mattie was cruising in the passing lane, overtaking several trucks that formed a sort of pickup caravan, and suddenly a big tractor trailer truck was bearing down on her. She could anticipate the feeling of the weight upon her as the monster truck gained speed halfway down the hill and drove right over her. The weight of the whole truck on her body, no pain, just the weight, which Mattie imagined would be worse.

"Where do you expect me to go!" Mattie wasn't talking to the driver, she was talking to the truck. She leaned into the steering wheel. "I'm going as fast as I can." She moved her car into the first narrow opening between two trucks in the right lane. "I hope you win," she called out as the truck zoomed past and then began to lose speed as he started up the long incline.

What gave that man such drive, so much impatience, such a need to be there right away? What was driving him? Had he grown up with an older brother who would bend his fingers back and torture him in other than the usual ways, or did he have a father who was never to be pleased, or a mother he was wooing still, as an old woman with a crinkly head of gray hair, or, perhaps, as a young blonde who chewed gum, talked fast, and would take any dare?

Or, maybe it was just the truck driver himself. Just his way. Written in his character. Character is fate. They always said that.

Mattie drifted back into the passing lane and looked out of the side window at the sky where it touched down to the trees. The sky, a dark gray now, not broken up in any way. Mattie had always taken a peculiar satisfaction in a cold, gray afternoon, and was not certain, did she love a day in late November best of all for its own sake or in memoriam, the steel-gray sky the form of memory. Memorial. Memento mori. Whatever that was. Mattie couldn't remember, if she ever knew. Something to do with death. Memory and death were great friends. They shared holidays. Memorial Day. Veterans Day. Mattie could remember when those holidays were quite the thing, with cemetery ceremonies and big parades with marching bands and soldiers.

When Mattie was a little girl there were parades for the least excuse, and her father made sure they never missed a single one. He would willingly drive twenty miles on country roads to stand on the corner by the drugstore in some little town, one of maybe forty fans, to watch a rag-tag junior-high-school band follow their drooping clarinets and trumpets down the

Main Street, pursued by two bass drums and a lone trombone, who were in turn being chased by a platoon of Brownie Scouts. Sprout Scouts her father called them.

Mattie's family were on some occasions the only people there who were not blood relations of parade participants. John Phillip Sousa was her father's Mozart, his favorite march the one that started, "Oh, the monkey wrapped his tail around the flagpole," and ended with a word of caution about being kind to web-footed friends and the ever-present possibility of a duck being somebody's mother.

Some parades were better than others. The ones on Veterans Day and Memorial Day took forty minutes, stretched out over two long miles, and ended up with everybody at the cemetery, where four different preachers prayed four different prayers to a single God, and Johnny Rosella sang, "Oh Danny boy, the pipes, the pipes are calling," and all the mothers—not the fathers, never them—who had lost sons in the war stood in a line and held the gold stars they had been given in trade for their lost boys. Then the band played "My Country 'tis of Thee" and everybody sang along and then they shot the Gold Star Mothers. Or that's what Mattie's father always called the repeating, fired salute, the mean, loud noise that pierced the morning air, always cool and just a little foggy, as though the VFW would have the weather be no other way.

For years, Mattie didn't understand her father's phrase was just a joke, his way of dealing with the part of the proceedings that surely must have sounded to his ear like the shots that killed his best friend Billy Laman, whose mother stood there every Veterans Day and held that silly wooden box with the gold star, the star that hung in her front window for forty years. Mattie's father would make jokes like calling the salute the moment when they shoot the Gold Star Mothers, and he would visit Billy Laman's mother every Mother's Day from 1944 until she died in 1983. He didn't miss one year. And every year he brought a leather purse until the woman must have had a closet full of them, somewhere. Thirty-nine black pocketbooks like Billy gave his mother just before he went away. Thirty-nine handwritten notes that said, "Happy Mother's Day. You'll always be my girl. Love, Your son, Billy."

Mattie's father kept faith for that long, and every Veterans Day he would tap Mattie on the shoulder and say, "Cover your ears. They're going to shoot the Gold Star Mothers." Maybe he said the joke so Mattie wouldn't be as frightened by the noise, maybe he said it for himself, or spoke the words out loud for Billy Laman, filling in his old friend's laugh, just like he signed his name each year on cards for Mother's Day.

No matter. For years Mattie took the words as truth, and worried the particulars for days. When she was very small, she thought the Gold Star Mothers were the ones who were indestructible. They fired guns right at them every year to prove it. A bit later, she had it worked out that the Gold Star Mothers did die, the rifles killed them dead, but they came back to life the next year just in time for the parade. It fit well with the cowboys who died every afternoon on *The Lone Ranger*, but who always rose to ride another day.

One year she got the idea that the Gold Star Mothers were being punished for not taking better care of their dead children, they were being shot for not protecting their dead sons. What kind of woman sends her child off to a place where she's certain shooting is. So it varied: Some years, nine-lives resurrection, some years, cruel punishment, and some years, pure and public proof what tough stuff a mother's made of. Here were a few more threads and snippets for a child to take to help work out what sort of thing a mother is. Mattie did want to know. Every year she stood a few feet closer to the Gold Star Mothers. A mother was a thing she did so want to understand.

Mattie shrugged her shoulders, shifted her weight from one side to the other, and leaned forward and then back again. She was cramped, in need of exercise. She might just pull over on the shoulder, put her four-way flasher on, and walk fifty yards up and down and back again, swinging her arms, getting the blood flowing. Or she could quick-step down into the ravine, and crunching brown and brittle branches underfoot, she could gather armloads of dried cattails to carry home. But Mattie saw a hobo in her mind, a 1930s hobo, hiding in the bracken, waiting for her there. He hadn't had a meal in days. He'd grab her keys and knock her down, and leave her stranded there alone. Then it would start to rain, a heavy rain, with lightning.

Mattie kept on driving. A walk would have been nice, but the lean, hungry stranger kept her on the road. Her fantasies, ideas spun from whole cloth, routinely kept her where she was, and made the prospect of action dangerous and not worth the risk. Fantasy. Her certain legacy. Mattie's whole family trafficked in fantasy, every one of them. It was a currency they understood. It was what Mattie thought to trade on even now.

As a child, going off to sleep at night, Mattie had a fantasy in which her grandfather, a man she had never seen, a man who was the reason Catholic blood coursed through her veins, and why her Presbyterian grandmother would cross herself whenever Mattie's father quit another job; the grandfather who lived in Harrisburg and called himself the Senator, and who, the ten-year-old Mattie believed, must surely have a lady friend, a blonde who wore tight satin dresses and red lipstick; Mattie, in between half-wakefulness and sleep, played over and again the fantasy that this grandfather would show up late one night, and sing out like the Irishman he was, "Get the children out of bed and dress them up. I'm taking you all out for dinner at a restaurant in Harrisburg" (a five hours' drive away), "and you can order anything you want."

Now that was real. A dinner, never had, in Harrisburg at 3 A.M. A meal half-dreamed a dozen nights, or maybe not even so many as that, that was real, more real certainly than the grandfather Mattie finally met, but only once and briefly when she was eighteen, the fantasy colliding with a stranger. That's what life was, a series of collisions, fantasy smashing head-on into reality.

Mattie heard the metal crunch. The crash. Her parents' car smashing straight into a tractor trailer truck.

What car had they been driving this morning? Nancy hadn't said. Nancy was so vague, so devoid of detail. She had always been that way. She had given Mattie not a detail for a day-long drive.

What cars did her parents own now? Mattie never could keep track. They usually had one big car—a living room on wheels with mushy suspension—and a small car. Some kind of Cadillac, and a tiny subcompact, painted red or white. They would be all right if they were driving the big car. If they had their seat belts on. Mattie had told them enough times to buckle up. She told them, sternly, every time she rode with either one of them.

And what were they doing out so early in the morning anyway? Nothing they couldn't have given a miss. People make so many unnecessary trips. There were so few places you actually needed to go, and if you smashed up on the way somewhere, you always realized that.

What if they were in the tiny tin toy? Small cars were stupid. Mattie remembered reading a report on car safety, and an expert said that he would guarantee in writing that at least the driver would be killed if you crashed, head-on, in a subcompact, going more than thirty miles an hour.

Mattie cruised at seventy.

At some point, sooner now than later, there was a certain kind of anticipating she would need to do. Some particular imagining of what awaited her in Granby. She needed to envision both, and one or the other, of her parents dead— each one in turn—before she reached her destination. The things you imagine hardly ever happen, or not ever in the way you picture them. To conjure tragedy was prophylactic. Mattie saw her parents dressed and dead, in satin-covered coffins in the viewing room of the Munroe-Babkin Funeral Home, the front room, lined all around with folding chairs, and baskets full of flowers, orange-pink gladiolas, roses, lilies, organ music, a continuous tape, playing something other than a song. Both her parents lying side by side, or against opposing walls, separated by the quiet mourners, by the soft hymns, and by death. Two caskets, two to view, which first? No. Her parents could not both be dead. Not both together. Certain things are too unlikely.

If this accident were serious, if it were as bad as it could be, then one of them would die. Just one. Which one? And who decides these things? What if it were Mattie? Her choice. Who would live, who die. What length of time would it require to arrive at that decision. Her parents both would be much older than they were today before she could sort that one out.

Okay. You've got five minutes. Who's to die? Which one will go on living? Four minutes. Choose. The mother who is the incomprehensible. The father who was always love but love far away, affection when he came upon you unexpectedly downtown, kisses on the crown of your head when he passed through the room where you sat watching television, ready "I love you"s at every seldom conversation. Three minutes. The one whose love you're sure of. The one whose love you still might win.

Hope springs eternal. It does in families. A mother dying will give birth to hope we christen If Only. And we say the baby's name a hundred times. If Only she had lived to have one more conversation, then I might have... then she might have...

Hope surfaces from underneath old garden furniture, it jumps out and surprises you at each anticipation of a three-day visit. You can point to it in photographs, in black and white. That's me. That's my mother. There in the lower corner, hope. Two minutes. Pick a name. Their fate, their lives, at least, are in your hands. Admit it. It is not a feeling unique in your experience. Even as a child you were no stranger to the idea that you held their happiness in your two hands, in your two little hands. One minute. It all hangs on what you say. Time's up.

ROUTE 80 EAST   NEXT EXIT. Mattie saw the sign and sat up straighter in the seat. This was the turnoff not to miss. Then it would be Route 80 until it seemed even the roadway would tire of itself and refuse to continue. Hours, Mattie would have hours now to think, and hours to anticipate them all, to hone herself down, not to something her family could find acceptable, but to something they could comprehend enough to criticize. And the criticism would feel like home, would be home. To ever move away so far that she could not be comprehended, to actually achieve the difference she had always felt inside; no, that would be too far away to ever go.

Mattie felt warm. She looked down at the temperature gauge as though it were a thermometer. Her eyes moved over to the gas gauge. Through the thick layer of old dust, it looked as though the red needle pointed far below the empty mark. Mattie took her thumb and rubbed the plastic clean. The needle didn't budge. She looked up and her eyes caught the sign for the turnoff to Route 80 East. Paul had filled the tank this week. How long had she been on the road? Mattie gripped the steering wheel, holding on so tightly that she could imagine it was her strength alone supporting upright not just the wheel itself but the entire steering column. She sat up very straight, turned off the radio and fan, as though to economize on fuel.

It had been years since Mattie had run out of gas. Not since before she married Paul. Paul kept track of things like fuel tanks, paid attention, glanced down at the gas gauge for no reason, filled the tank before it got to empty. Mattie did not often think to notice.

Also, Mattie did not like to stop for gas. It was an interference, an interruption on your way from home to there, or coming back again. She hated to stop for milk or the dry cleaning. Mattie liked to get where she was going, traveling in a straight, unbroken line. To stop along the way, even out of necessity, felt random and haphazard.

Two or three times Mattie had run out of gas in town, within walking distance of a service station or a telephone. Only once did she remember running out of gas out on the highway, on an interstate. It had been early in the morning, and a man about fifty-five, dressed in a business suit, had stopped by her stalled car and driven her to the next town and back again with a can of gas. Mattie never would have done that for a stranger. In fact, she was pretty sure that she would no longer accept that kind of help from someone she did not know. She used to do a lot of things she would not consider doing now. She had placed an ad in the personals section of a local newspaper in order to meet men, and so had met, and married, Paul, and had two sons. Things went that way. You could never anticipate the length of slender tentacles that sprung from any isolated act, any random whim.

You do a lot of things when you are on your own. You take rides to service stations with men you don't know, and advertise for spouses, and you run off to Europe solo. Then you get married, and so many things are dangerous. You have children and you have to be so careful.

The car felt as though it were losing power, yet when Mattie pushed gently on the accelerator, the indicator moved from forty-five to fifty. As she crested the hill, she took her foot off the gas and let it coast. The car felt logy and out of control at the same time. Mattie saw an exit sign too far away to read.

SUNBURY   LANCASTER   ROUTE 37 SOUTH   2 MILES

Close enough to walk, if she had to. Mattie slowed to forty and reached into the side compartment of her purse, fishing out two lipsticks. Without looking in the mirror, she put on the Iced Pink Frosting first, then the Baked Coral Sun, and blotted her lips on a flier for a takeout submarine shop.

SUNBURY   LANCASTER   ROUTE 37 SOUTH   1 MILE

Mattie could walk a mile in fifteen minutes. She would welcome the exercise. It would feel good to be out and moving. She took the exit, coming to a full stop at the sign, and turning left toward town.

A steep hill ran all the way into town, with a concrete wall, six or eight feet high, which looked to be the only thing that kept the steep, grassy slopes from falling down across the roadway. Blocks and blocks of houses, perched so high; at first, tarpaper shingles in brown tweed, then gray or yellow slate asbestos shingles, then woodframe houses, painted in misguided pinks and fading apple green. Mattie could imagine worn chenille bedspreads on iron beds, and flowered gray linoleum in every bedroom in every house.

Who would build so many houses clinging to the sides of hills? Mattie could not conjure the condition that would make it reasonable. She knew full well that driving one mile and a quarter out of town, the landscape would evolve to flat and level fields where houses would seem natural and well-supported.

Someone hadn't been thinking. A lot of people hadn't been. These people who set up their lives, so all day, every move they made would have to take a hill into consideration, and they would need to make certain accommodations at every turn, with all their comings and their goings.

CHAPTER THREE

A T THE BOTTOM of the hill, Mattie could see two signs for gas stations. A rusted Texaco red ring that would bring big money in an antique shop in Woodstock, Vermont, and a new, lighted, white rectangle Mobil sign. Mattie picked the Mobil. Who knew the history of the gas across the street? It may have been delivered with the sign.

"Fill it, please," Mattie said. "Regular." She couldn't remember if she was expected to say something about lead. *High test* and *regular* were the only words that came to mind. She wasn't sure if they were still in fashion. It had been a long time since Mattie had bought gas. Paul must have been taking care of it for longer than she had thought. He always did self-serve. Mattie hated self-serve.

"Is there a restroom?" Mattie's body felt older when she

tried to take it out of the car than when she had put it in.

"Key's inside. Right inside the door. On your right. About eye level. Black and gold football helmet on the chain. Steelers."

"Thanks." Mattie crossed the parking lot on legs that seemed forgetful, rubbery.

Inside the building there was no key. There was no hook. Mattie stood in the middle of the floor, surveying every wall. The room was completely empty, but for soot and grime on every surface, counters, walls and floors and ceiling.

The outside door opened, and a gray-haired, well-groomed woman came in carrying a large white bakery box, a coffee thermos pitcher patterned with blue ducks, and a large shopping bag. The woman's shoes were brand new.

In health class, in the seventh grade, Mattie's teacher, Mr. Hawkins, told his class that the only sure way to spot newlyweds at airports was by looking at their shoes. Researchers had discovered that the newly married wore new shoes with a statistically not insignificant frequency, though why researchers or seventh-graders or anybody else should want to pick out all the newlyweds in airports Mr. Hawkins did not say. And then the bell rang. Bells were always ringing in the seventh grade. It was how you knew when you were finished learning one thing and were ready for the next, how you separated your facts: like new shoes in airports always mean wedding bells, as distinct from the idea that an isosceles triangle has properties it shares with no other triangle, and only certain rectangles.

"My, this is such a special day," the woman in the new shoes said. She looked like no one's bride. "May I help you?" The thin, starched woman took from her bag a felt-backed, paisley, plastic tablecloth and spread it out on the widest of the countertops.

"The restroom key," Mattie said. She wondered what was in the white box and who it might be for. A bakery box will always give rise to shameless interest. The woman pulled off her smooth red kid gloves.

"The restroom key. It's on a chain with a football helmet on one end."

"I know," Mattie said.

"Well, let's see." The woman scowled at the four walls, each in turn. "Please excuse this room. This is our first day. I wanted to get a cleaning service in but Jaycee wouldn't hear of it. He makes such a thing of independence. Always did. At five years old he was packing his own lunchbox. If you can imagine. We could ask him for the key, but I hate to disturb him when he's in the middle of a sale, especially his first day."

Mattie turned to look at the young man, who was bent over a plastic podium beside the gas pump writing something down.

"A charge card," the woman said.

Mattie could read the writing on the pastry box. FRANKIES. *Frank J. Barzalone Prop. 418 Main Street*, and two different phone numbers.

"Oh, may I offer you some pastry?" The woman broke the string with one fierce snap.

"Oh, no thank you." Mattie planned to say yes in a minute. The young man opened the door.

"Mom, you promised." He did not look like someone who packed his own lunchbox. Mattie spied the miniature black and gold helmet hanging from the pocket of his jeans.

"Jaycee, just a little snack, dear, for customers. This

woman—I'm sorry, I don't know your name. I'm Lydia. Lydia Wilder. And this is my son, Jason. He's the new owner."

"Mattie. Mattie Welsh."

"Well then, Miss Welsh, what will you have?" The woman pulled a Blue Willow pattern plate from her bag and began to arrange the sugar-and-cinnamon-coated-shapes. She took out several Styrofoam cups and a carton of light cream.

"Don't tell me," the woman said, "I know. Cream is poison, and Styrofoam probably means the end of life as we know it on this planet, but I've had these cups at home forever, and sooner or later someone will throw them away, if not in my lifetime, then after that. So this just speeds up the inevitable."

"Mom, you promised." Jaycee left the building in a huff.

"He's got the key," Mattie said.

"Oh, well, give him just a minute to calm down. He does fly off the handle, I'll say it even if he's mine. He did as a boy. Then an hour or two later he will be back hanging around at the periphery, and finally in the smallest voice you'll hear, 'I'm sorry, Mom.' You could set your watch by it."

"I don't think I'll be here that long," Mattie said.

At that moment Jaycee stuck his head inside the door. "I looked under the hood," he said to Mattie, making a production of not acknowledging his mother's existence. "Your water cable's loose. Take me two minutes to get a new clamp on."

"Oh, thanks," Mattie said. "The key." She pointed to the football helmet dangling from his pocket.

"See," Lydia Wilder said. "He's really quite kind underneath it all," as though car repairs were acts of charity, not commerce.

Mattie brought the key back after she used the unlocked restroom.

"No one knows Jaycee like I do," Lydia said. Mattie wondered if she'd missed a connector while she was out. "A mother knows her child."

Mattie had two light French breakfast muffins and a cup of strong black tea while Jaycee clamped water cables and his mother rearranged refreshments. Standing by the cloudy window, trying to piece out designs and shapes across the hillside covered in crown vetch, Mattie wondered if maybe she were missing out, always letting Paul fill up the tank.

"Oh, will you just look at that." Lydia Wilder moved to stand in front of the oversize window, her pointed finger no doubt invisible behind the dirty glass. "The way some people go out in public."

Mattie looked in the direction of the gas pump to see a skinny woman with a sunken face and long, straggly hair, in earnest conversation with Jaycee. She stood beside a beat-up boat of an old car with three or four small children playing in the backseat, crawling over to the front seat, two at a time.

"I hope she isn't planning to distract Jaycee from working on your car." As Lydia Wilder spoke, Jaycee turned from the woman and walked toward the garage, as though in response to his mother's voice, as though the two of them could converse from any distance, no matter how far away.

"Her battery's shot," Jaycee said as he walked through the door. "She's got exactly four bucks and no credit cards. She bought a dollar's worth of gas, not even a full gallon, and then when she went to leave, the thing wouldn't start. It won't take a jump. What am I supposed to do?" he asked his mother with a certain edge of accusation. He might be twenty-five or thirty, but he was such a teenager.

"Everyone has credit cards," Lydia Wilder said. "Ask her again."

"Mom." Jaycee's voice was annoying in several different ways.

"Do as I say," the dragon woman told her son. "Tell her she has no choice. She'll come up with something. People don't go about totally devoid of all resources. All she needs is a credit card."

"Here." Mattie held out a silver VISA card, the rainbow-colored holograph on the plastic flashing in the strong fluorescent light.

"I'm not finished with your car yet," Jaycee said.

"No," Mattie said. "It's for the woman's battery. I want you to charge it to my card, and I want a decent battery with a long life expectancy—and no one in North America will fault you if you give me your opening-day special discount on the price."

"Let me talk to the woman." Jaycee was clearly warming to the notion of his first real sale.

"No," Mattie said. "I want you to tell her that you found a battery here left by the last owner. Say it's of no use to you. Make up something. Just tell her there's no charge."

"Oh, miss," Lydia Wilder said. "We can't let you pay for it."

"She can do what she wants." Now that a solution was on offer, Jaycee seemed prepared to rekindle his quarrel with his mother.

"Well, look at that car and all those children," Lydia Wilder said. "The woman *needs* to get herself more organized."

"The woman *needs* a fucking battery," Mattie said.

The room was no longer empty. Suddenly it was full to bursting with Lydia Wilder's shock and indignation and

Jaycee's clear delight. Mattie said the word *fuck* about once a year, and when she did, it always seemed just right. Ah, the power of language. One word can whip a whole conversation into shape, turn a roomful of people toward useful occupation.

Jaycee took Mattie's credit card and left the garage. Lydia Wilder started rearranging muffins. Mattie stepped outside and sat down on a low concrete wall.

People who were poor, especially if they had children, always summoned Mattie's mother lightning-speed to mind, where she would stand looking genuinely sympathetic, even kind. Mattie's mother always was partial to poor people being herself poor, albeit intermittently, for the first forty or fifty years of her life. Mattie had always believed that poverty had formed her mother, fashioning her fixed inferiority, serving as the underpinning of her certain and defining insecurity. In the world her mother knew, having money meant that you were okay, acceptable, worth chatting with in public. Being poor meant you were made of lesser stuff, shoddy goods fashioned into some inferior product. And it seemed as though the die was cast so early on that, no matter how much cash might later come your way, there was no upgrading to a better self.

Mattie's parents had received three large and very welcome inheritances from three different aunts at well-timed intervals. Mattie did not pretend to know the cash amounts. The only exact figures she had been privy to were on the debit side. Starting when she was eight or nine her father used to tell her every cent the family owed, how much, to whom, and for how long, and that there was no money, none at all, to pay them. She couldn't say today what she had been expected to do with the information. At the time she had assumed she was somehow expected to come up with the cash. What was a child to think?

But windfalls were a different and entirely secret matter. Mattie's great-aunt who lived in Cleveland died and the summer after that her mother bought two houses, little houses to be sure, but houses all the same. Her mother fixed them up and rented them for thirty years. So she must have gotten some useful amount of cash from Cleveland. When the relatives who died were on her father's side, the telltale signs of any legacy would be late-model Cadillacs and trips to visit Methodist missionaries in Chile and trips to Hawaii to visit no one in particular. By that time Mattie was grown and gone away. She just got postcards from places with foreign foliage and once, out of the blue, the four-slot toaster that had been collecting crumbs in her kitchen for a quarter of a century.

So. Want and plenty. Mostly want, in Mattie's day. Hence her mother's penchant for the poor. She was nicer to poor people than to anybody else, especially rich people, and most particularly to rich people who were also relatives, except of course when they were dead and wills were read and then Mattie's mother said, "Well, she's in a far better place," and she would be entirely willing to let go her grip on poverty, perceived or real, for as long as the money lasted, which with Mattie's father was never all that long. Then things would get back to "money can't buy happiness" in no time at all, and they would be reestablishing their blood-brotherhood with the poor, whom you do indeed have with you always. Jesus said that when that world-class hypocrite Judas Iscariot started taking issue with Mary Magdalene's expenditure of a little cash for foot oil. And Jesus got the next part right as well, telling Mary Magdalene that wherever the story would be told, her gesture would be a key part of the telling, and two thousand years later there she was, dead center in the story. It could lead a person to consider that good deeds might have a longer shelf life than you think.

CHAPTER FOUR

MATTIE STARTED TO turn left, reconsidered, backed up, backed up farther, turned the wheel. A man pulling into the parking lot called out his window, "Hey, lady. Make up your mind. What do you want?"

"What do I want?" Mattie made a sharp right onto the roadway and gunned it. "What do I want, you say." Mattie checked her rearview mirror just in case. "What do I want? I want what every other woman wants."

Mattie liked the way her voice sounded, important in the empty car, on the empty highway. What does every other woman want? Mattie scratched her cheek. She wants a stream-lined thought life and devoted, funny–never–boring friends, and an art form she excels in that only a few people in the United States have ever heard of, and she wants a life diagram, a map, a signpost in her living room with a single arrow pointing in only one direction. She wants to give away her vacuum cleaner and her makeup bag, and live in a commune with sheep and goats and a lot of wholesome-looking people doing art projects, and she wants to be by herself some part of every day. She wants the satisfaction of knowing she is in the middle of a difficult, but worthwhile, project that a lot of people, including herself, care whether or not she finishes. She wants to be comfortable in a large-brimmed straw hat, and wear it in Italy climbing the steep, steep hills in Orvieto, and take it off to swill Campari and feel not much of anything at about four o'clock every afternoon. She wants to cook outrageous meals, have large dinner parties, and write serious fiction. She wants to be slightly mystical, or spiritual at least, and play the viola, well, with a small chamber group that practices on Friday nights. She wants to be a former Olympic high jumper and do polished figure skating on the frozen pond up by the college and she wants to do none of these things, but something else entirely. She wants what she imagines other women have.

Mattie caught the sign for 80 East and took the entrance ramp at forty.

It is a myth that everyone is speeding off toward a destination thought out in advance, cruising at sixty or sixty-five on an open highway with all the windows down, the warm breeze lifting up your spirits and your perfumed hair, Beach Boys surfing music on the radio, turned up loud. A woman's life is more a thicket than a superhighway, with bramble bushes in the way that take you off for entire days at a time in other directions than the ones you had in mind. Bramble bushes that impede your progress, scratch your hands and face, and send you running upstairs for the iodine and Band-Aids.

Bramble bushes that propel you toward hardware stores for hatchets and brush cutters and other tools that seem like a good idea at the time, that send you to the rental stores to rent a chain saw just as the manager is locking the front door to close up for the day, and saying he's sorry, but he's late as it is for the dentist, has a wicked toothache that refuses to give way even to cocaine. Life is that kind of thicket. The kind that makes a move from point A to point B seem like something best begun right after breakfast, with a clear head and a length of heavy twine. Then add in that deciding point B is where you will want to be once you arrive, and that it isn't until you are thirty-nine that you start to consider point C makes more sense the whole way around, and you began to get a measure of the exact perimeter of the thicket, feel the early autumn squishiness of fall leaves underneath your feet, and see just how far off it is possible to be in calculating the interval of time from twilight until nightfall.

Once back on the highway, Mattie felt resourceful. She had played it just right. She was almost certain that she had read somewhere that you should try, periodically, to clear your tank of all the old gas, flush it out completely, get a whole new start.

Mattie tried the radio again and found a country-and-western station. She turned the volume up. The song was about a man who said he was alone, and sickened to his very depths because he'd lost his loving power, and there was only one woman on this earth who could bring his manhood back again, and she was gone for good. The song ended with little question about the outcome, and they went right into the next song. Mattie guessed it would be tricky to know what commercial to play right after that.

The next song was about a woman who had made up her

mind not to be trampled on by life, not ever again. Not to be hog-tied, walked on, lied to, stood up, passed over, flung aside, no, not a single, solitary time again. She sounded like she meant it.

Mattie only listened to country-and-western music when she was in the car, and then only when she was alone, but she enjoyed it. She liked the stories and the people, and how everyone was always trying to get a new cut on things.

Mattie could remember when she hadn't liked it, when she had hated the very idea.

"I used to go to all your mother's dances." The remembered words echoed through the car. How Mattie had cringed at those words, had shrugged or scowled or made a puzzled face when people said them to her as a child. Mattie's mother had been a country music singer. She had dropped out of school at fifteen, after the ninth grade. (Mattie had always known this as the major failing, *the* regret, the underpinning of her mother's shame, the reason she went looking through her days for slights at which to take offense, the ready-made excuse demanding that she be forgiven all.) By age sixteen, Mattie's mother was singing on the radio, and by twenty, she had her own band. Hillbilly music. (The words *country* and *western* had not been coupled yet.) Hillbilly, the name of embarrassment when Mattie was in second grade. Mattie wondered how had she learned so early the disdain, the certain prejudice, when she could not have even named a single song her mother sang, all over Pennsylvania and New York, as far away as Buffalo, driving weekends in her new, enormous Buick, rating extra ration coupons for gasoline, all through the war years. Every bit of it remarkable for a young girl who made the whole thing happen by herself. So who had instructed Mattie in disdain?

Her mother's career had been short lived. By the time
Mattie was a toddler, her mother had been *saved*, and was convicted—that was the word—that dancing, and by association,
music anyone could dance to, was a sin, and she sang only
hymns. Who knows, Mattie thought, maybe dancing was a sin.
Maybe it still is. Only how could anyone have been so sure, so
convicted, that they could condemn Mattie to years of sitting on
a bench in phys ed class while all the other girls square danced,
condemn her to a banquet on prom night, sponsored by the
church, where all the girls wore prom gowns and corsages to
eat dinner.

So dancing was a sin, along with everything else anyone
might think to do for recreation in Granby, Pennsylvania, in
1962, and hillbilly music was beneath contempt. Her family
might have marketed the past so differently. They might have
told the child, "This is the four-hundred-dollar raccoon coat
your mother wore when she was famous. These are her gui-
tars, all made by Gibson. These are the photographs, her auto-
graph, her leather boots, her newspaper clippings."

As it was, Mattie had come upon these artifacts, hidden in
the back of the deep closet she and Nancy had pretended was
a cave.

Mattie punched the buttons on the radio. The only other
station she could pick up was playing something that sounded
like Bartók. Mattie hated Bartók. She turned it off and looked
around as though the landscape might hold interest not at
once apparent. She decided not. It was a barren stretch that
might have driven Bartók to his discord, if only in some
attempt to alleviate monotony. Better strident screeches than
one long note held four full beats, repeating endlessly. Maybe.
Mattie wasn't sure; she'd never had the choice. It seemed now

that her life at home had been made up in some measure of both, the screeches and monotony, alternating in a pattern that was not predictable. But then what were other people's families like when they were home alone? You only really knew what went on at your house and at the houses that you read about in novels.

Mattie had always carried the idea that other people's lives were different from her own, substantially different in ways that would be difficult to imagine or to learn about. She once had a fantasy of telling people she was writing an article, maybe a book, about how people spend their time, and asking would they keep a daily log, if it wasn't too much trouble, noting all the things they did and when, for seven days.

Sometime later, she would ask "What do you do?"

She would say it when the air felt light, and people seemed at ease, or sometimes when there was a dry spot in the conversation.

"What do you and Silas do?" she would say.

Paul told her once that other people only did the same things she did. Mattie did not think that likely.

And it was harder, too, to find out about other people if you were a private sort yourself. Growing up, Mattie had been curious, wondering what the other girls would stand about in giggling clumps to whisper and gyrate about. She would walk by close enough to overhear, but it would be *boy, clothes, hair, homework, parents* talk. She would assume they changed the subject when they saw her coming. When she was older, in her twenties, it had surprised her what passed for conversation among women when they were in groups. Men were a different story, setting up their own camps on the borders and periphery of any real exchange.

At one point, Mattie had tried dropping in on neighbors,

appearing unexpected in the middle of the afternoon. But she would only find them out at something ordinary, creating tall piles of folded sweaters, moving dishes, chopping large green peppers, reading Lillian Vernon catalogues and drinking luke-warm coffee, standing by the stove. Things she did herself. She was not going to surprise the truth from anyone that way.

Sunbury 47 miles   York 86 miles   rest area 2 miles

"Rest Area" in Pennsylvania could mean anything from a large, substantial-looking red-brick building beside a stand of Coke machines to a paved cutoff long enough for twenty cars, not counting trucks, featuring a single picnic table. Mattie would rather eat in the car. She fumbled in the canvas bag she had gotten as a giveaway from a book club, and fished out a chunk of cheese and half of a loaf of pumpernickel bread.

Mattie liked eating while she drove. She liked eating while she was doing something else besides. She had read a list of dieting tips once in a women's magazine that said you should eat only while sitting down, and you should never read or do anything else while eating. That would be the diet for Mattie. She would weigh sixty-seven pounds. She would eat once a week, confined to those conditions. Women's magazines were full of advice like that.

"I don't know why you buy those things," Paul said every time Mattie reported her worst fears had been confirmed in *Women's Journal.* She would buy the magazines at the super-market checkout counter for the recipes and makeovers; but Mattie didn't cook things she hadn't cooked before, and more often than not she preferred the "before" pictures in the makeovers, so she would end up reading "Twelve Diseases You May Not Know You Have," "Deer Ticks: Danger in Your Own

Backyard," or "Variety of Sudden Infant Death Syndrome Strikes Teens," and scare herself silly. Not much of a stretch.

Fright. Her legacy, the trait Mattie had carried away with her when she left Franklin Avenue forever; carried in one piece, entire and intact. Fear. From observation and from lessons. Home-instruction in being afraid. It's not that hard to teach fright to a child who in his mind has ready access to catastrophe.

"The seeds inside green peppers are poisonous. Eat one and you're dead." Her mother speaking.

"If your tooth aches bad enough, the pain will make you go insane." Her voice again.

Insanity. One of the biggies. The oracles left nothing to the child's imagination. At the age of eight, Mattie's greatest fear was that she would need brain surgery, and she had overhead her parents in the kitchen over coffee describing the operation, saying that because it was your brain, you needed to be thinking, your thoughts running at full tilt, during the operation, your brain working at capacity, even as some white-coat sliced away. They couldn't knock you out; they couldn't give you so much as an aspirin.

Teaching terror by instruction, fear by demonstration. Here, watch. I'll show you. Or don't watch. It won't make any difference. Danger's in the air.

Sunbury 37 miles   York 76 miles   next rest area 40 miles

The idea of forty miles alerted Mattie's bladder. She would never make it. Sunbury. York. Sunbury wasn't on the way to Granby. Sunbury was east. Not west. Mattie drove on several minutes before there was a sign.

80 east

She was driving east, not west. Ever since she stopped for gas, or no before that, she had been traveling away from, not closer to. For what, an hour, maybe closer to two, she had been driving—no doubt over the speed limit—heading in the wrong direction.

CHAPTER FIVE

NEXT EXIT   HAYTON 47 SOUTH   PALMER 4 MILES
Palmer. Mattie hadn't been to Palmer since she was eight
years old. Mattie had attended most of the fourth grade in
Palmer, one stop along the way, as her parents hopscotched
across Pennsylvania, jumping down to Florida twice, in search
of something new. What, Mattie couldn't say. Whatever it was,
they never found it and finally moved back to Granby in
retreat. Mattie wondered if her changing schools once or twice
a grade had helped create the awkward, sometimes odd out-
sider she felt herself to be. It certainly hadn't interfered with
the development of her self-consciousness. It takes a sturdy
child indeed to be the new kid every blessed year.

Mattie drove past the Hayton exit. She might as well go on

to Palmer; it was just as close. She could call Nancy from there and find out about her parents. She might have driven on, straight through without calling, had she not lost her way, gotten off her course. She would call from Palmer, tell Nancy she was running late, offer some explanation. Then she could find a restroom, maybe get a bite to eat, some coffee. She stuffed the bread and Cheddar cheese back in her bag.

Mattie had had the idea of going back to Palmer for years, only it wasn't on the way to anywhere. This would be her chance. Mattie loved the idea of returning after so many years, like making a surprise visit to your fourth grade. She had told Paul once the reason everyone should move away from home was so that you could hang on to it the way that it had been. She said that if you go on living in the place where you grew up, it changes and you see the changes every day, and you lose what was there without much noticing. They raze your elementary school and put up four matching ranch houses on the site, and by the time the shrubs around the front have taken hold, you have all but forgotten that the houses weren't always there.

But if you move away and come back just to visit, then you see what's missing right away, and feel indignant at the barbarity and go off again with the whole thing in your mind almost exactly as it's always been.

Mattie could remember specific sidewalk cracks in Palmer. There was no experience of the town to intervene, obscure the memory; 1957 was preserved intact. For that one year, Mattie lived in the right side of a two-family house, the front porch a level concrete-slab extension of the sidewalk, a configuration which permitted Mattie's father, on one occasion, to bring a horse named Cookie, a full-size tan mare, into the front hallway—at least, the front half of the mare—and to call out to Mattie's mother, "Come out here. There's someone here to see you."

A horse needs to appear in the front hall so few times to make you wonder always, as you pick up the towel to dry your hands, and smooth your apron and your hair, make you wonder, as you walk toward the front door, still holding the tea towel, wonder who, or maybe what, awaits you there. Expectation is that way, it thrives on one-time happenings and widely scattered hints and promptings.

Mattie could remember well that house in Palmer, the house they lived in for one year, the house with the wire-fenced backyard where Mattie planted poppy seeds and hundreds of red poppies grew, and when she carried armloads of the red flowers marching with the Brownies in the Memorial Day parade, the rich red petals fell away, till Mattie was left holding only stems on her arrival at the cemetery. She wrote a poem called "Among My Garden Plants Doth Grow the Joy of All My Sorrow and Woe" that night about one poppy in particular.

That house. The house with the steep rocky driveway at the side, where Nancy, who had seen the first seat belts somewhere, chained her brother Eddie to his tricycle with the link chain from the swing set and pushed him down the hill; the house where in the upstairs hallway Nancy had told Eddie he could fly if he jumped off the top of the mahogany armoire they rented with the house.

Mattie and Nancy had parts in the operetta at the grade school there and dressed in gauzy, colored cheesecloth as The Leaf and The Breeze. Their father said it was a pure case of typecasting if he ever saw one, and for years afterward would on occasion, use these stage names for the girls. "Tell the Leaf and the Breeze to come for supper, on the double."

Mattie had a club that year that met one time in the front parlor of that house, with weekly dues five cents, to be kept in the slotted record cabinet in a glass jar Mattie had covered with pink and mint-green crepe paper, rolled tightly into strings and glued around the jar to cover it completely. Mattie could remember knowing how to make so many things.

The club: a lackluster affair, and only for girls, not like the fan clubs—one for Elvis, Elvis Presley they said then, and one for Pat Boone—clubs that met after school with records and dancing. Mattie had gone one time to the Pat Boone club, even though she knew she couldn't dance, with a boy called Spencer Hepner. Mattie had five boyfriends that year in Palmer, four of whom were cousins, Hepners all, and Jimmy someone, who gave Mattie a circle pin he found and said "damn" out loud at baseball games.

And there had been girlfriends, too, in Palmer, like Paula Rumbarger, who because her father worked for the railroad, couldn't receive calls on the telephone—an explanation obscure even then, to them who took so much on faith. Mattie had to go down to Paula's house if she wanted to talk to her on the phone, and then, if Paula's father wasn't home, she would call Mattie back.

Paula Rumbarger, and a friend who lived on Main Street, across from a store that sold embroidery thread in every color, and buttons, singly and on cards of six, a friend whose name was gone but whose father used to walk Mattie home, for safety, if she stayed until after dark. But Mattie was more frightened of the father than of the unintroduced and always walked several steps ahead of him, until her house came into view and she would break into a dead run.

Mattie felt a pang. She'd like to see those little girls again, like to meet the women they had been turned into.

Come to think of it, you could probably fill up whole empty sections of your life resurrecting all the people that you used to know, telephoning friends from every stage of your life, explaining who was calling—as many times as necessary—fetching memory from far places, deciding whom to call and where to meet and whether you should pack a picnic lunch, or maybe just a thermos jug of tea with milk and sugar and two kitchen cups to carry down to the big rocks by the river, or leave the tea unmade and meet at some fancy restaurant you could not have afforded when the friendship was first wonderful and so brand new. Then you could spend more time deciding who will pay and who will leave the tip and what to talk about, and in the end deciding who has been the most surprising, who has been the most surprised, realizing who must have still been liking you for the whole while, or who had maybe never liked you that much in the first place.

But there was no one here today to call, no people, only stories, shadows of the players. On Main Street Mattie had lost a five-dollar bill one night on the way to the store for someone's mother. That night she did not know what she would do if she couldn't find it. She didn't know today.

So many details survived: a tiny dead mouse lying in the grass on a Sunday afternoon when Mattie went out to someone's farm with people who were visiting from West Virginia, a 1957 Chevy, the first one, on Main Street, red and white, the smell of horn oil on her trumpet, roller skates, scuffed white buck shoes.

Mattie tilted the rearview mirror down to check her hair. In Palmer, when she was eight years old, she had cut her own bangs, a jagged fringe above a face that could have done with better, smiling with a tight-cheek smile in black-and-white school pictures. The photographs were all in color now, and all the children, every one, was photographed to look well groomed—well bred, for that matter—healthy, and likely to be successful in school sports and in later life.

In color. In the fourth grade in Palmer, Mattie had saved her money to buy a pair of two-tone, bright pink pedal pushers with a fuchsia sash that she wore to school with a new turquoise turtleneck. The first time, the only time, she wore them, Candy Clark—that was her name—asked Mattie had she thought today was Halloween, and Scotty Aucker laughed out loud and for long enough to make his name a memory thirty-six years later. And where was Scotty Aucker this afternoon? And who exactly cared?

Mattie had been oblivious to the strip of fast food places, invisible when you weren't contemplating pulling into one, camouflaged by their enormous signs and garish shapes and colors. She was surprised at the first stoplight to see she had arrived at the main intersection, the only intersection, in Palmer. She was certain this was it. She waited at the light, and saw a parking spot just ahead. She parked the car, got out, creaking-stiff, and as she put money in the meter saw a phone booth a few feet away. She was inside the booth, the thin directory in her hand, before she realized she was calling a number she already knew, calling Nancy who would tell her something (tell her what?) about her parents, whom she had spent five or six hours driving toward, and then away from, somehow managing to do so little wondering, so much wool-gathering. She, who worried every small event, who would throw up a smoke screen of anxiety and wild imagining at the slightest invitation, had driven hours, not imagining in any reasoned way.

"Hey, lady, you gonna' use the phone or what?"

A thin young man in a black leather jacket with silver studs spoke to Mattie through the door. Maybe this was Scotty Aucker. Too young. Maybe this was Scotty Aucker's son. Mattie was always expecting to run into someone whom she knew. Someone who knew her. She always tried to be prepared for it.

"No. You go ahead," Mattie said.

She stepped out of the phone booth but then stood by, a short distance away, impatient while he made his call. It seemed he was calling for a ride, but the person he was calling, Bill, was not immediately willing.

Mattie nodded to the boy as he stepped out.

"Okay then?" Mattie said.

She needed to talk, to hear her voice and someone else's in reply, to warm up, before she made her phone call. The boy scowled and put both hands in his pockets as he walked away, a little bounce as he touched down on each foot, not a new bounce, Mattie thought, but one learned long ago.

She stepped back into the booth and took out all the coins in her wallet, spreading them across the dusty ledge. There must be three or four dollars; Mattie never spent her change.

Mattie dialed 0 and Nancy's area code and number.

"Please deposit one dollar and sixty cents for the first three minutes."

Mattie would have liked to say something in reply, but she wasn't sure the voice was not a recording, or some computer sound, not a voice at all.

"Hello."

"Hello. Nancy? This is Mattie. I'm having a little trouble.

I'm on my way. I called to tell you I'll be later than I thought. How are Mother and Dad? Are they okay?"

"Dad's fine. A couple broken ribs is all. But Mattie, oh, Mattie. It's Mother."

What? Mattie thought. What's the worst? Paralyzed, blind, both arms broken, both legs.

"She's gone, Mattie. Mum's gone."

Gone where? Mattie couldn't think of where she would go.

"They tried to save her." Nancy sounded like an old, old woman. Or a child.

"What?" Mattie said.

"They tried everything. The steering wheel crushed something inside of her, and she bled in there."

"I need to find a bathroom. I'm in Palmer."

"Palmer? What are you doing in Palmer? That's way over by Harrisburg."

"I know," Mattie said.

"Well, you couldn't have done anything if you were here. She wouldn't even have known. Oh, Mattie, she's gone."

"I was on my way. I was coming," Mattie said.

"David and Eddie are here. Don't drive fast. There's nothing you can do. They gave Dad a lot of drugs to knock him out, and they say he won't really be awake till morning. Are Paul and the boys there with you?"

"No, I'm alone," Mattie said. "I'm all by myself. I can't even call Paul now. He's in surgery. We decided he shouldn't cancel. He's coming down tomorrow with the boys."

Mattie walked away from the phone booth to a bench nearby. It was right on the sidewalk on Main Street. A weird place for a bench. Mattie didn't remember seeing it before. Had this bench been here when she was eight? Mattie tried to think.

Things were so confused. They had altered the whole scene, shrunk Main Street down, and put up buildings willy-nilly, randomly, in places where they didn't fit. Mattie sat down on the bench. She breathed in and out through her mouth; the air would go as far as her back teeth, then out again. Her lungs were empty; they were not accepting air. Mattie wasn't sure if she had just called Nancy, or if she still had to make the call. She couldn't think of any way of finding out. Mattie couldn't remember if she turned the dryer on before she left the house this morning. Paul was there. He would turn it off while things were still a little damp. He always did that. Mattie hated it. She liked the clothes to be so hot and dry that when you took them from the dryer you imagined they were sterilized.

She had somehow always thought her father would die first. She had had lots of fantasies of his dying, of his being gone. She had always felt she needed to be prepared for it, not taken by surprise.

But her mother. Mattie felt perplexed. She had never once before today thought about her mother's dying, thought about her mother dead. Mattie's mother had talked about her own and everybody else's death for years. "Your mother's been dying since 1944," her father joked. Over the decades she had lost a certain credibility.

When Mattie was in the sixth grade, her mother took her up the shaky, pull-down ladder to the attic. It was a hot September afternoon, the attic stuffed with dry, stale heat, full up with dust motes and the disremembered leavings of two generations' lifetimes.

"I want to show you where I keep the Christmas tree ornaments," Mattie's mother said. "Just in case I'm dead by Christmas."

(How fierce and nagging are the fears that make a mother say that to a child. How heavy and how everyday her fright. How few people must she have to tell her terror to.)

And that was thirty Christmas trees ago, and nearly every Christmas was her last. As far back as anybody could remember, Mattie's mother had been been decorating trees and dying. You don't expect a person who talks about death that way to ever really go.

Mattie remembered reading that a famous painter had said that his depression was the organizing influence in his life. In Mattie's family that job went to death. Someone was at every moment near death's door, (Mattie's grandmother had devoted fifteen years to her own demise), it was what they talked about, what passed as conversation. Mattie could not recall her mother, or *her* mother, having any other hobbies.

Maybe the preoccupation came from more than fear, perhaps it offered more than just an organizing structure. If every day there's some near miss, a close call, an almost, not quite, a narrow, or a fat, escape, it lends a certain drama to what might otherwise be a succession of pretty ordinary days. Even a ditch-water dull life dangled over the edge of a perilous ravine will hold some interest for its owner.

But now in this moment, Mattie had no plan, no way to be. How do you deal with losing someone you haven't got ahold of yet, someone who has always slipped through your fingers, someone who was never there.

When Mattie was growing up, her mother was always at home. She hardly ever left the house, except to go to church and to the grocery store. And yet hard as she tried, Mattie could not recall her mother's presence, she could not remember her, except for a handful of scant impressions:

scrubbing floors, ironing shirts and dresses, washing dishes. There, not there.

Oh, she had been there in ridicule, Mattie thought. There, in ridicule and disapproval and in sudden anger, anger unexpected, always a surprise, however much you worked up an anticipation; walking through the kitchen on your guard, coming in from play, but never thoughtlessly. No matter, you could not anticipate.

Mattie could remember she had dawdled one day walking home from church.

"You made me wait." Her mother in the bedroom, changing before Sunday dinner, screaming, lashing out with the bra she had just taken off, swinging the strap and catching Mattie across the cheek with the curled metal fastener, making a clean cut.

Family anger goes a hundred different ways. There is the sudden kind that cuts a slash across a little girl's cheek, there is the kind that can destroy you, cut your heart out, leave you bleeding on the floor, (Nancy's kind), and there's the kind that just makes a lot of noise and breaks all the windows in the house just to let a little breeze in. That kind is a royal mess to clean up, but it can clear the air like you wouldn't believe.

It is no simple thing. *Cause* is always waylayed, interfered with, on its way to *effect*. A brother knocks a sister down out in the kitchen late at night when everybody else is fast asleep, and she can call the police and have them come and write it down, or she can die or she can go on living. She can wake her father and her mother and half the neighborhood, or she can say, "I can't believe you," and go off to bed. People in a family can do awful things to one another, and then afterward a choice gets made. It happens all the time.

Mattie had known sudden anger punctuating months and weeks and days of nothing to report. Neither harm nor good. Not even words to tuck away. She must have spoken, must have been attended to, in the times in between. Only, Mattie couldn't call it back, couldn't hear the tone of voice or any of the words.

And now, these last years, her mother vague and fuzzy around the edges and, Mattie thought, perhaps the whole way through. There was an elusive I-don't-know that was her retreat, her barricade against even the easy questions.

"Well, I don't know," she said, spoken in a voice suggesting she was not sure of even that. Perhaps she didn't know, or else she fuzzed out before she would give vent unwittingly to a position. There was no one home to hate. No one substantial enough to even make a case against. No one to stand trial, to face the charges, unless opposing counsel would, at this late date, accept a plea of vacant.

But then, a trial to judge a life would be a tricky thing. Tape record anybody's life, or better yet, get twenty years on video, (a child will memorize a mother just that way), and a brand-new lawyer could convict a saint.

So. Had this woman been a mother who was good enough? There seemed to be some need of summing up the sketchy evidence at hand. Had she been a good-enough mother? That was the fancy, eighty-five-dollars-an-hour phrase that shrinks used: the good-enough mother, the one who gave her offspring just enough of what was needed to get by, and not a penny's worth more. The term always struck Mattie as the last word in inferiority. A good-enough husband. A good-enough loaf of bread. A good-enough life. Who wants that, for pity sakes?

The last time Mattie had visited at home—it had been

almost a year now—one afternoon she and her mother had been left alone when everybody else went off somewhere. As soon as they had gone, Mattie's mother jumped up from the woven, plastic-slat chaise longue in the backyard. "I have to do that lasagne," she said.

She had only to warm it up for dinner, and it couldn't have been much after two o'clock. Mattie followed her in through the back door, out into the kitchen. Mattie prowled the pantry. It was hot.

"Do you ever buy the generic brand of oregano?" Her mother said those words.

Questions like that enraged Mattie, filled her up with a remembered, full-fueled fury at conversation crafted to keep her at a distance, conversation so desultory and innocent seeming, but planted with land mines Mattie tripped on every time.

"What kind of idiotic question is that?" Mattie wanted to scream. "Why don't you ever talk to me?"

"I buy fresh oregano," she never would have said, would know it for the veiled assault, the implied criticism, of her mother and her way of life it would be taken for. She could decode the silence that would follow such a declaration, even if she were unconscious, could condense the silence to a phrase someone could embroider, work in needlepoint, and frame and hang up on the wall: *To Be Yourself (if that includes buying fresh oregano, and then saying so) Is To Hurt Your Mother,* and in wool or cotton thread of a contrasting color: *Everything You Do Implies A Criticism Of Everything You Do Not Do.*

Mattie's separate acts, her very statements of them, were the embers that smoldered in the walls, involving all the wiring in the house, upstairs and down, that never broke to flame but charcoaled struts and beams and rafters.

Mattie knew the rules: She could not say what she thought or felt ("I don't like spiced apples." "I feel bad when you keep bringing up my divorce all the time."), much less could she be a separate person, sitting in a separate chair, with her own history and construction. Mattie knew it well, had learned it early on, long before she could have put the thing in words. But she chafed and fretted, wished it other than it was. Mattie focused the better part of herself on regretting what had never been. It wasn't every minute, every day, but it was there to click into; it was never beyond reach.

And Mattie, who would never say, "I buy fresh oregano," would burst out from time to time with damnings, accusations that would not be said out loud in families where more usual words were not routinely disallowed.

"Why don't you show any interest in your grandchildren, like normal people do?"

"Why couldn't you admit you never loved me?"

"Now, Mattie, you know that isn't true. You must be over-tired, dear."

And once, one time, when after years of silence, Mattie resurrected old sins of her parents, gave them all their proper names, Mattie's mother said, "Have you talked to your father about this?"

Score one for Momma. She was absolutely right. Mattie's father was forgiven all—his sudden temper, even beatings— while Mattie's mother could not be forgiven gestures, intimations, attributed intent. Mattie would concede this puzzle part of it, and say out loud, if only to herself, she hoped her sons would be more forgiving than she was. Her mother and her father could have done each one the same thing; and one would be damned, and one forgiven, even understood.

So why *had* she never said anything to her father about what he had done? Mattie toed an oak root raised above the surface of the ground, a gnarled vein on an ancient hand. Why had she not confronted her father with his sins?

Because he would be hurt. That's why. Because he bled when he was cut. He could be hurt. And Mattie tried to hurt her mother. Had she ever succeeded, ever gotten through? She had no idea.

An old woman carrying a bulging plastic shopping bag, and a large purse and an umbrella, was heading toward Mattie's bench. Mattie glowered, stared her down. The woman paused but walked on by. It was cold sitting here. Mattie was glad that it was cold.

It had been hot that day last summer. Very hot.

"Do you ever buy the generic brand of oregano?" her mother said.

"What do you mean?" Mattie said.

"Well, this is the generic brand. I buy their oregano some-times. That's what this one is."

"Tell me about your life." Mattie's answer.

"What do you mean?"

"Well, your childhood. I've never heard you mention it."

"Well, I guess it never came up. There isn't much to tell."

"So, tell me what there is," Mattie said.

"Well, we lived on a farm, and my mother and my father worked hard. We didn't have much."

That much Mattie knew.

"What were your parents like?"

"Well, they worked hard. You work hard on a farm."

Mattie knew that too.

"Why did you drop out of school?"

"I didn't have the money for the bus. It cost fifty cents a week, plus I didn't have shoes to walk the two miles to the bus."

"I never knew that," Mattie said.

"Well," her mother said. "I wanted to sing. I wanted to sing on the radio. So I started taking guitar lessons once a week in Punxsy."

"How much did that cost?"

"Fifty cents a week."

"So where did you get the money?"

"Oh, Mum got it for me some way. Grandma Campe was a wonderful woman. She loved you very much."

"I have such mixed-up memories of her. I asked her once to help me with my spelling words. I was in second grade, and she asked me all different words that weren't on my list. She tried to get me to spell *horse* and *lightning* and *potato*. She always made me feel confused. So much went on I never understood."

"That's a real shame, Mattie. My mother was such a fine woman; it's a shame you must remember her that way."

Her voice leveled, moved dead center into the groove of serious offense taken, injury suffered at Mattie's hand. Injury so sudden and so grand, the victim has the right of way.

Mattie shivered. She should be up and moving. She walked over to the parking meter by the car and put in another dime, even though she still had fifteen minutes. She should walk somewhere, around this courthouse she remembered, around this tiny square the years had so reduced in scale, shrunk down almost to miniature. Mattie walked up to the door of the courthouse. It was open.

"Excuse me, could you please tell me where to find a ladies' room?" she asked the woman behind the counter in the first office with an open door.

"Upstairs, two flights, on your left."

Mattie didn't believe the only bathroom in the place was on the third floor. She was out of breath as she pulled open the heavy door and went inside the dark oak-paneled ladies' room, antique in every detail, as though modernization had never made it up the stairs. With all the rich, warm wood the room looked genteel; the atmosphere was like a library, or a special room in a museum, closed to the public except for Tuesday afternoons from one to four.

Mattie studied her face in the metal spotted mirror as she washed her hands. She wet the sliver of a bar of soap, dried and brittle, very old, perhaps original equipment in the court-house, and Mattie remembered her mother had taken a Red Cross first-aid class once when Mattie was a little girl. She had come home late that night and told Mattie she had learned that hand soap can kill any germ there is. No germ known to man can live long on a bar of soap. Mattie wondered what the Red Cross said today.

Her mother had taken a course. The idea pleased Mattie. Her mother had taken a course and had come home with a piece of information, no matter how spurious. She had taken a course, and Mattie had remembered it. What else might there be to draw forth from this abandoned well?

Mattie pushed open the heavy door. Who put such a barrier on the ladies' room? Not a lady. Not a woman. Mattie started down the stairs, stopping on the first landing by the window. She could see her empty bench. Who would dare sit there? She smiled a smile that made her feel a tiny pinpoint of pain deep inside her ear.

There was an imagined conversation playing in her head, an ancient conversation she played over and again. Mattie always started it:

"You hurt me," Mattie said.

"You hurt me," her mother said.

"I can't reach you."

"I can't reach you."

"You are cold."

"You are cold."

"You don't know me."

"You don't know me."

"You don't want to know me."

"You don't want to know me."

"You always liked Nancy best."

"You always liked Daddy best."

"You never wanted me."

"That's not true, Mattie. I love you."

No answer.

"I can't talk to you," Mattie would imagine saying.

"You can talk to me. I'm your mother. I love you."

The show stopper.

"You never liked my friends," Mattie would go on. "You ridiculed them and me. You never let me be myself. You took offense if I was me. You took it as a direct assault on you if I read books or had ideas or liked other people."

"I used to dress you up," her mother would reply, "when you were four or five and take you downtown for a soda in the afternoon. You were so grown up."

"No, I wasn't. I was five years old. I was a child. For years taken together I was someone growing up, and even then, inside those little dresses, sitting up beside you on a swivel stool, I was trying to be me."

"You were so grown up. So sweet. I loved you very much."

The brick wall.

"The only way to be myself," Mattie would plow on, "to be a self at all and not a lump of gray putty, was to fight my way free, to signal my intentions angrily; fence in a space for me, the boundaries all the way around, barbed wire and sticks and bristles. You took my ideas as assaults, my little likes and dislikes as betrayals and disloyalty."

No answer.

No one there.

And standing now beside the third-floor window in the Susquehanna County Courthouse, an imagined Mattie regaling an imagined mother, she saw the conversation as some carefully crafted assault. How could she permit this conversation to play over in her head at this moment? How could she play any other?

Mattie stared blankly out the window. Could her mother overhear her thoughts now that she was dead, a spirit in the atmosphere, a presence in the metal skies? Would she be with Mattie everywhere forever now? Had they sprung the trap?

People write to Ann Landers to say their deepest regret is that they'll never see their mother (or their father or their sister) alive again. The first time it had occurred to Mattie that both she and her mother had serious intentions of winding up in heaven, albeit heavens of two very different sorts, the idea had panicked Mattie. They would be together forever. She would never get away. An eternity. *The* eternity. Never separate. Some therapist would be licking her chops over that one.

Mattie used to be a therapist. A psychiatric social worker. Complete with third-party payments and a tasteful office and patients who came twice a week and on time. But she wasn't a therapist anymore. Blame it on transference. Mattie had been pregnant, sitting with a patient, a lawyer, a woman respected in her field, even by people who knew her. "I would like to take a knife and cut open your belly and kill your baby," she had said. Transference. Feelings for another person in another time transferred to Mattie. Why me? she had wondered that afternoon, after the patient had left her office, she feeling unaccountably relieved. Why me? It wasn't the lawyer. It was everyone. The whole idea of it. Such an unnatural way of being with other people, trafficking in transference. Mattie thought if she ever went back to doing therapy again, she would go back as the dispenser of advice. "You should pick up your life and run with it." "Divorce her." "Stop sniveling." "Marry him." "Get pregnant." "Leave town."

Mattie had had a dream not long ago about a therapist who came to your house and did the dishes, cleaned up, did the ironing, while you talked. A graying, sturdy woman, who smelled of lavender soap and wore a pin shaped like a turtle on her lapel and carried in her purse a smooth clean cotton apron. The woman folded laundry and never missed a word.

"I'll just change the sheets," the woman said, "and you can tell me all about it." By the time she woke up, Mattie felt that she could tell this woman anything.

CHAPTER SIX

MATTIE NEEDED TO be eating. She needed to be drinking coffee. All the years Mattie was growing up, her mother would leave unfinished cups of coffee sitting on the counter, on end tables, in the bedroom, and she sipped them through the day. Just in the past year or two, Mattie had begun to do the same thing. Mattie needed coffee, now.

She had a clear view of all the buildings across the street. There was a coffee shop, spelled without any extra letters. A good sign. It looked the sort of place where you could get good everything, except perhaps for coffee. (That would be thin and dark, and not too hot to drink right down, but tasting like the flavor and the color had been superimposed.) But everything else would be wonderful. Mattie could conjure a four-color poster on the wall above the sizzling grill, the photograph, a hamburger with chips and crinkled pickle circles, surreal beside a pink milkshake with two tall straws. Then, on a plate on the counter in front of an old man, the real thing: the white bun, soft and not too fresh, the patty, cooked to perfection, the cheese, American, and lettuce, and tomato, tasting like tomato even in the month of November. But you wouldn't have to order the cheeseburger. You could order anything. Their fried eggs came out every time just like what God must have had in mind when he invented chickens.

Pierson's Coffee Shop was the only business on the block besides Joe's Bar and Grill that looked as though it had escaped renovation. There was no evidence on the exterior of either place suggesting that someone with a lot of time and cash and big ideas had had a go at it. The benefactors of indifference or original ownership, both Pierson's and Joe's stood just as Mattie might have seen them from the backseat of the green Buick, gazing out of the side window as they drove away from Palmer on that June day in 1958, drove away forever, Mattie must have thought riding out of town, never thinking for a second that she might come back to meet bad news on Main Street on this distant afternoon. Mattie liked to think that she remembered the two businesses just as they stood, but her memories of Palmer were confined to three tight blocks, each one with sidewalks made of lifting yellow bricks, and to the house that they had rented furnished with antiques, the house with seven rocking chairs.

That house where she and Nancy shared a room and Nancy stretched a string across the middle of the room, saying she would beat Mattie to a pulp—her words—if she put one foot on Nancy's side, which had the only door. That house where Mattie's little brother, Eddie, bit the neighbor's dog, or so went the story they took with them when they moved away.

Mattie looked across the street at Joe's Bar and Grill, its neon sign that must glow orange or blue at night, a cold, black outline in the afternoon. Joe's didn't look familiar, didn't summon an association. But then, why should Mattie remember a bar? Bars were forbidden places. Drinking was a sin.

To her certain knowledge, Mattie's father had never tasted alcohol. Her mother wouldn't even buy rum-flavored LifeSavers. Mattie had put sherry in a beef stew her parents raved about when they visited her in Buffalo, when she was a newlywed the first time around. She had proved exactly nothing to herself, except perhaps that little things can make you feel as bad as big things.

Mattie spun around as though she had just remembered an appointment, and went quickly down the two broad flights of stairs, not holding on, and left the courthouse. Mattie realized that when she was eight and lived in Palmer, she had not one time walked inside this building. And it was one short block from where she'd lived, two minutes from her front-stoop play. She could have come here anytime, wearing school clothes, looking purposeful. Things can be close at hand and far beyond your reach at the same time.

Back then, Mattie's world had been so small, so surely bounded, so confined and circumscribed. A dark closed space, a cave, it seemed sometimes when she looked back, when she went back, in feelings, went back, often, without caution, though she knew full well that cave was darker than would be accounted for by just the keeping out of light. The cave was full of darkness that was a thing in its own right, darkness and black rock floors, trick-slippery or worse, missing altogether.

Sometimes for the space of a whole season, Mattie would be back there, mired in her years of growing up, more often there than in the present. Even walking down the main street where she would conduct the business of her days, those years would come back to her, as memory, or as the old self-consciousness, which would be all of a sudden, everywhere, spit-shined, and still entirely service-worthy.

It wasn't always. Mattie could sometimes walk for miles on a November afternoon, not noticing herself at all. It was just that it would come back to her when it would, and she would be guilty and not decorative or coordinated, and everyone would care.

Feelings are memory, Mattie's first therapist was wont to say, and these were feelings that sold well when Mattie was a little girl, already cautious of clothes and hair and schoolyard conversation. And that wasn't even where it all began. Those were just the reinforcements, like the metal taps on blue leather strap shoes in the seventh grade—metal taps that would preserve the heels and toes long after the shoes no longer fit, metal taps that could wake the dead, alert them you were on your way. Only reinforcements. Mattie knew her awkwardness was cast in stone well before memory came along.

So, Mattie thought, now crossing Main Street at a quick step, why do I go back there? Why does back there come to me? Mattie had friends who seemed to visit childhood not at all. It was as though it had all happened long ago, to someone else, or hadn't really been that bad; or they had projects, paying jobs, and lots of stress; they sat on three committees, or had a hobby in the basement. It seemed it was all in the present with these people.

Mattie felt it was all past with her, that she could see the fifties much more clearly than she saw today.

Mattie had a friend who said once she would like to walk up to herself at the age of seven, see the little girl that she was then, and put her arms around her, and say to her, "I love you. You're a fine, fine girl. There's nothing wrong with you at all." Mattie could imagine herself enacting such a scene: not being convincing, not being convinced.

These feeling memories, Mattie wondered, will I teach them to my children? Give me sons, she had always said. (A daughter of mine wouldn't stand a chance.) Sons, swift, strong, and unafraid, may they outdistance me.

It occurred to Mattie, as if for the first time, that these days, these years now, would be the childhood of her children, the years they would remember without taking thought, the rascal images that would inform their silent hours, the ones they would recall as old men puttering in drab brown kitchens, the days remembered sitting on a bench somewhere, alone or with someone.

"Ahh," Mattie sighed aloud. I'm so caught up back there, still ducking bat wingspreads, rubbing my bare arms against the cave's black damp, how can I think to fashion a remembrance for them. I guess until I thought it out, I must have believed that it would be my childhood they would be remembering.

It seemed to Mattie, standing on the sidewalk there, the idea was not strange at all.

She looked around, surveyed the street, as if for confirmation or argument. She was feeling very odd, had no idea why. Pierson's Coffee Shop. Joe's Bar and Grill. Mattie turned back around to face the street again. She stopped just short of standing up on tiptoe, peering with a purpose that would have been convincing, had anyone been there to see. Posing. She was buying time. She was standing slightly closer to Joe's than to Pierson's.

For as long as she could remember, Mattie had wanted to go to a place like Joe's, alone, her shoulder bag in place supporting the whole weight of one arm, casual, offhand. She would walk in in the middle of the afternoon, enter the dim interior, the safe enclosure that admitted every confidence, that made reflexive allowances for human failing and was open to everyone and every story that they had to tell, but open to the light not ever, and not to judgment either. Acceptance, unconditional. You could wear anything to Joe's. Could order what you liked. Draft beer and a shot, a glass of water, a bag of sour-cream-and-onion chips, champagne—well, maybe not champagne.

Mattie thought she comprehended in her bones the clientele and the philosophy of Joe's. She felt as though she had spent a hundred dusky afternoons sitting on a stool, the plastic cover of the seat in slits, her legs wrapped back around each side of the metal pole, or sitting over in the corner at a tiny wobbly wooden table, warming herself by the light of several pinks that shone from the old jukebox no one ever played in the middle of the day. She never spoke when she was there, she never wanted to. She sipped heavy sherry, checking the rim of the thick wineglass for sharp edges. She would stare at the odd light that framed worn dark red velvet curtains at the single window; the odd light you must see from this one table if you were to take it in at all. The only other occupants sat singly, murmuring underneath the ball game on the radio, if they ever spoke at all.

Mattie had a sudden feeling like a loss that she had never once, not ever, been inside a place like Joe's. She turned and marched up to the door, as though there were some chance she might be denied admittance, as though if she didn't go in right this minute she might not ever make it.

∞

Inside, Mattie blinked. The light was perfect. As it should be. Only, for a moment, Mattie couldn't see a thing.

"Can I help you, miss?" The voice came from the center of the darkness.

She thinks I want directions or change for the parking meter, Mattie thought.

"Do you by any chance have coffee?" Mattie said.

Mattie moved in the direction of the voice.

"Next door. Over to Pierson's. That's where you want to be."

Mattie sat down on a stool, the plastic smooth across the seat.

"No, here is where I want to be," Mattie said. "Do you have beer?"

"Now, there you're in luck," the woman said. "We just happen to have got us a new shipment in this afternoon."

All of a sudden Mattie realized she wanted nothing so much as a beer. A Sam Adams Double Bock, and a thick pastrami sandwich on pumpernickel with some serious mustard.

She felt jazzed up and heavily sedated. She should eat.

Palmer. She calculated.

"A Bud, please." She thought it had come out just right. Mattie was feeling very much at home. "This is my first time here."

"Is that a fact now. I coulda' swore you was one of our

regulars." The woman put the beer down in front of Mattie. "I could tell by your accent, honey, you was just passin' through on your way to someplace else."

"My accent. Why, I live just down the road a piece." The words, the inflection, the way of speaking was second nature to Mattie, maybe first nature to be exact. She could call up Pennsylvania talk, the language, the diction, the decided woman's whine without taking thought. In fact, she switched dialects reflexively when talking to her Aunt Alma or her mother's nephew, Larry (her cousin Larry, actually; she always thought of him as her mother's nephew—a new cut on "once-removed").

"I'd like to know what accent you would be referring to," Mattie said. "I come from Hagerstown, and all my people, too."

"And I'm to be elected Miss America by Bert Parks in Atlantic City come September," the bartender said.

The beer tasted foamy and it wasn't really cold.

"I happen to have moved to Massachusetts," Mattie said.

"The *Mayflower* and all that." The woman spoke as though the Pilgrims were still getting off the boat.

"No, it's not like that. It's just like here. Driving the Massachusetts Turnpike you would think you were on Route Eighty. It's practically the same everywhere. Malls taking over, McDonald's arches framing every tree. Every place is pretty much like every other place."

"Right, and I am the missus of Michael Jackson."

Mattie wanted to look around. She had come in to soak up the atmosphere, not attempt a conversation with this woman. It occurred to Mattie, she might have thought an old man quaint were he to speak the words this woman uttered. Mattie wanted to move over to a table, the Formica glistening even in half light, but she knew the woman would take it personally.

Women do. She felt trapped, and the beer was making her sleepy. She would need to go next door for coffee.

"Where is everyone?" Mattie said.

"Who'd you have in mind?"

"Oh, no one in particular. I just figured..."

"Everybody figures. That's the problem with the world. No one takes it as it comes. No one leaves the house in the morning without a full-fledged set of expectancies."

Mattie's wrist jerked. She almost dropped her glass. She set it gently on the bar—a child's careful gesture.

"I did used to live here," Mattie said.

"That gives you a common interest with a lot of people. Used to doesn't count. It's the ones as stick it out you wanna' know about. I'd got out, got out in a minute, same as you, but I was sixteen years old and on my own. Worked over to the button factory, and by the time I was eighteen I was married, with a baby. I was never fond of babies. Oh, you love your own, don't misunderstand me, but babies, in general and on the street, I never had what you would call a particular interest in. Four babies in five years, and I was here for good. Of course, I loved them." The woman attacked the counter with a wet cloth and some purpose.

"And of course, I did *not* love them the same way. That's another myth they put about." She made it sound fairly well organized. "They tell you you love 'em all the same, but I have yet to meet a parent who does. There's always one that makes you think they made a Xerox copy of yourself, only with better chances, and that's the one you love something fierce. That's the one that gets piano lessons and leather cowgirl boots and sunglasses and table manners. The one who misses school a lot; and that's the one you think is your salvation. Then ten years go by, and ten more, and she don't resemble what you had in mind at all. I'm not saying that you write her off. That kinda' blind attachment's always there."

Mattie watched as the woman began to wash tall glasses, standing each one gently on the thin towel she spread out on the counter.

"Then, the one comes after that has colic, spits up, picky what he eats and what he lets you dress him in, and he turns out chubby, roly-poly, sits on your lap a lot, and buys you perfume you can smell across the room when he's eleven, using his own money, and you like that one the best of all. With him it's not so complicated. That's the one that grows up grateful to you. Want another beer?"

"Why not." Mattie's whole face felt relaxed. Her jaw muscles felt longer than usual, and made of some stretchy material. She would be humming along if there were a song playing on the jukebox now.

"And take one for yourself," she said.

Mattie had seen it done a million times in movies, on TV. She had read the scene in countless mystery novels: a person buys a drink and says to the bartender, "And take one for yourself." Mattie had always wondered how the bartender drank with everyone who happened in with a little extra cash or an expansive disposition. In the course of one movie, a bartender might get offered half a dozen drinks. He would be too drunk to pour, much less make change—forget about his bladder— and Mattie had never seen or heard about a bartender who was intoxicated. They always looked and acted like the nurses in starched white who handed out the pills but never swallowed any down themselves.

The woman opened a bottle of Budweiser for herself,

holding it between her hands like she was warming it. Mattie wondered just how many drinks she had been treated to. Mattie took a long swig. Beer didn't need to be ice cold. They served it at body temperature in England, and they had pubs that had been in business seven hundred years. Americans were too particular.

"So you had four children," Mattie surfaced with the words. "That's your family?"

"That's all that I'm aware of," the woman said. "See, a man could say that, and you'd think he was a gay blade in his day, although my Jeannie tells me they've changed around the meaning of gay; that it's not just cheerful anymore."

She took a long, slow drink.

"Four children. Two boys, two girls, though there are days that make you wonder what the good Lord had in His mind when He invented the idea of female children. Not that He pulled any punches in the beginning. He told Eve straight out before He showed her to the door in the Garden of Eden that it wasn't gonna' be no picnic, but you want a couple daughters to convince you whereof He was speaking."

The woman turned to put her empty bottle under the counter.

"At first," she said, "you dress 'em up in little dresses with white embroidered ankle socks with lace around the top, and shiny patent-leather shoes, and you think you've got a little doll on your hands. Then they get on for three and a half and start in with moods, and that goes on, as far as I can tell, until they're dead. Now, you take a boy. He even starts to feel a mood come on and he's out of the house, slamming the screen door off its hinges, gone so fast you'd never know what hit you. And he plays some kinda' ball eight months a year, and if he has a set of his own disappointments, who would know. Oh, you hear your boy was in a fight with that no good Deans boy, and one time he comes home with a new twelve-function pocket knife you know he did not trade for cash, but as for moods—moods girls have every morning before breakfast— boys don't stand still long enough for them to hit."

"Do you like your daughters now?" Mattie was working her way around to asking if there might be anything to eat.

"Well, since you seem to want to know, I'll tell you. I do not seriously imagine that I would be friends with either one of them if we was not blood relatives."

"Same with me," Mattie said.

"You don't look old enough to have grown daughters."

"Oh, no. I don't mean my children. I would always want to be friends with them. No, I mean I wouldn't be friends with my sister, or with my mother, either, if she were alive."

"How long since she's passed away?"

"A few years," Mattie said.

You can't blurt out the news your mother has just died this afternoon. People don't know what to do with it. Mattie could remember having lunch with her friend Michael on a bench outside the science building at Amherst College on the afternoon his mother died. Mattie hadn't known about it until she showed up with two veggie pocket sandwiches with feta cheese and salad dressing, and two Cokes, and two limp sour pickles, and Michael said, "My mother died at eight o'clock this morning," and the sandwiches were already there; so they unwrapped them, and two friends came by, and they laughed and joked and told stories about people they all knew, and when Michael went to put the papers in the trash, Mattie told the two men Michael's mother had just died, and they both acted stiff and peculiar, and left like they were in some suddenly remembered hurry. You couldn't say to people that your mother had just died. It made them behave in other than helpful ways.

Your circumstance might be brand new, but you are still you. Say you just fainted. Sitting on the supermarket floor, beside the meat counter, shivering, when it occurs to you, sitting there surrounded by eight or ten strangers, two of whom will turn out to be registered nurses, and all of whom will be curious and alert, distracted from the boredom you have called them from, you are still you. Sitting, palpitating, going in and out of crisp, clear thinking and ideas, and sweating, heart pounding, turning beet red (those words spoken by a nurse who should know better), thinking what a thing it is to die there with your puzzled children, neither one above the age of six, die where you had never thought of dying, sitting there, you are not changed from the crisp, efficient woman with a list who worked the aisles systematically only minutes earlier, comparing prices, reading entire lists of ingredients, choosing lemon peel for flavoring over MSG. You are not changed sitting on the supermarket floor that will seem to you cleaner than the floors at home, there, waiting for the two men in blue shirts with BRAYTON FIRE DEPARTMENT written on the pockets, the two men who will transport you in an ambulance. You are still exactly you, but everyone will treat you otherwise.

You are still you if your father is convicted of a serious crime after you are grown and gone, or if you win a large amount of cash, or if you're robbed while waiting for a bus in broad daylight. You are still the same you if your husband gets another woman pregnant, and with twins; although no one will treat you as if that were the case. If you get a painless but unsightly rash that covers ninety percent of your body, people will treat you differently. Or if you stand out in the snow in slippers and your overcoat and watch your house burn down, you will for months after that be responded to in a new way.

You say, "My mother just died," and everyone will make twelve imaginative assumptions and handle you accordingly, and if you faint in the supermarket on a Tuesday morning, everyone will treat you in some peculiar way as you are carried on a stretcher down Aisle 10—plastic wrap and dog food, and less crowded usually—when all the while, inside, you are still only the same you, and nothing like their idea of you at all.

Mattie was getting fidgety. She needed to find the ladies' room, but she didn't want to go there by herself. She thought it was a good idea to stick together here. The telephone rang, and the woman picked it up while it was ringing the first time. She would catch the caller unaware. Mattie guessed from the woman's words and manner that it was a daughter on the phone. Mattie spun around on her stool, her back now to the bar.

"No, you don't know what I want," the woman said into the telephone.

Oh, yes I do, Mattie spoke in her mind, spoke to her own mother, whom she propped up in a wooden chair against the back wall, over by the outline of a jukebox. I know exactly what you want, Mattie thought, or what you wanted. You'd be surprised how clearly I have understood your needs. You wanted demonstration that somebody cared. You wanted taking care of, pampering. You, whose job description was giver, mother. You wanted to be the child—the center of attention— the pretty little girl that everyone fussed over and adored.

That's all. Nothing peculiar about that. Only unattainable. Not ideally suited if you've set yourself up with a house and husband and four children. Poor planning. Your besetting sin.

Mattie was certain her mother had resented Mattie's appearing just when life was shaping up so well: fame, money, work, love, praise, all things no little girl would choose to trade in on a three-room apartment, cold in winter, hot in summer, dingy in between, and a husband, dedicated, unreliable, by fits and starts, and the needy infant stranger for her sole companion, the only life that filled some weeks and days. Mattie always had been sure her mother hadn't welcomed the idea of her. The concept of a little life to be responsible for. Yes, definitely, poor planning.

But Mattie could remember her mother, four children later, standing in the dimly shaded, summer shadows of the afternoon, upstairs in her bedroom, by the bureau, shrugging, saying, "I can't figure how you're supposed to use this diaphragm. I don't even understand the idea of it."

Hapless. The word had been invented for her mother. So much of life had come as a surprise.

Mattie noticed the sign that said LADIES, printed in red ink on a card with curling edges. It didn't seem so far away. She thought she would be able to hear the woman's voice even through the door. Mattie stood up and crossed the floor.

When Mattie came out of the restroom, the woman was combing her hair, peering into the small white-framed mirror as if she weren't immediately certain she recognized the face.

"We're leaving for the airport in a little bit. I don't like to throw you out, but I'm going to have to close up the place. Jake, the night man, will be here at six." As though Mattie might like to go and cool her heels somewhere, and come back later for another lukewarm beer. The woman recombed one whole section of her hair, though it seemed to Mattie that the comb made no impression.

"You're just going to close up. Lock up in the middle of the afternoon." Mattie, the injured party.

"You got it. Daughter's flying in by plane to Harrisburg. Gets in at four forty-seven, and me and my other girl, Babette, will pick her up. My Babette drives. The one we're going to get works in a hospital in New York City. An anesthetist. Not everybody can pronounce that. In fact, most people get it wrong, leave out the 'the' or add an extra part."

"So, she's a nurse," Mattie said.

"No. That's what I'm telling you. She's a doctor. Puts people out. One needle and they're dead to the world. She says sometimes they talk when they're under, it has the effect of what you might call a truth serum. They spill the beans when they're half in and half out. Jeannie used to tell us all kinds of stories about stuff that happened. She doesn't anymore, but when she was first learning the ropes, she'd tell us all of the particulars. Not just the crazy things the patients say when they're unconscious but the stuff the operating doctors do. She said one time the doctor, the assistant to the operating one, went out to the gents' while they were taking out somebody's gall bladder, which I don't even see how anybody could think about doing, let alone actually do."

The woman had her compact out and was powdering her nose and chin and then each cheek, reminding Mattie of the way Catholics and certain Episcopalians cross themselves, in church, or on airplanes, or on hearing certain kinds of news. Mattie couldn't always figure the exact cue they were responding to; the stimuli seemed to vary. Mattie studied people when they did it. No two people did it the same way. Some used a fist and some a thumb and some an open hand. Mattie always meant to ask someone about it. It seemed a soothing sort of exercise.

"All that blood and gore," the woman's voice was deep.

"What?" Mattie felt as though someone had pushed the pause button on the conversation.

"The blood and gore," the woman said, and hit FAST FORWARD. "Ugh. I mean just the idea of all that blood and guts in the operating room gives me the willies. The first spurt of red blood shooting at the ceiling and I'd be outa there, I'll tell you that, and guts all over the place. It's hard to think that any child of mine could sit by and watch that stuff." The woman's comb was back in action. "But you'd have to know my Jeannie. She's a cool customer, if you'd ever want to see one. And smart. She coulda' been a regular doctor. She was smart as a whip. I don't know where she picked up her brains. She didn't take after me. I'd say she wasn't a bit like any one of her own people. She has a way of being nice as pie when she wants to, but then she can cut you cold. She's not married. Divorced. It's hard for me that both my girls went through a divorce, but my Babette, she's married now to Jim Burns over to the paper plant, got two nice kids, and there's Jeannie, all on her own. You can't tell me she's happy, I don't care how much she makes. She's going off overseas all the time. What fun is that, if that's all you got? I don't know. You try to raise 'em the best you know how, and look what happens. Well, you take your time and finish up your beer." The woman disappeared into the ladies' room.

CHAPTER SEVEN

SOMETHING WAS WRONG.

Mattie held two fingers to her wrist, and once she picked up the beat, she counted for fifteen seconds by the clock. Eighteen. Eighteen beats times four was thirty-six plus thirty-six. Her pulse was seventy-two. It felt more like two hundred. She could have taken her pulse just by laying her hand on her chest, her heart was pounding so. What if she had a heart attack in Palmer. She didn't think there was even a hospital in town. There didn't used to be. When she was traveling with Paul and the boys, Mattie always liked it if they passed a big hospital sign right before they found a motel.

The outside door opened, and Mattie spun around on her stool.

"Hi." The new arrival walked in, put her several bags down on the counter, and went behind the bar to get a beer. "Do you know where Bea is?"

"She's in the restroom, if Bea is the woman who works here." Mattie always bristled at familiarity from strangers.

"Yeah, she is. She's my mother. You're not from around here."

"No. I'm not," Mattie said.

"I don't know what we're going to do. We were supposed to pick up my sister in Harrisburg, at the airport there, and I go out to start my Chevy after I finished with my shopping, and nothing. The engine's dead. I called everybody I could think of, and my husband and my dad are off at work and nobody else is home. Jeannie'll have to take a bus. Not that it'll hurt her. Like maybe a doctor's too good to ride a bus or something. She's a doctor. But I don't know what else we can do."

"About what?" Bea crossed the room. Her bangs and one side of her hair were wet and kinky like a brand-new permanent. It made the dry part look unnaturally puffed up. "Do about what?"

"My car won't start. I went out after shopping to start it up, and nothing. Engine dead, I guess is the problem, and I called everybody but no one's home. I don't know what we're supposed to do."

"Good Lord. We got no way to get word to Jeannie on the airplane. Maybe we could call the airport and leave her a message and then after we didn't show up she'd go ask someone if there was any messages for her. She never liked the bus."

"I'll take you," Mattie said.

"What?" Bea and Babette used one inflection.

"I'll take you," Mattie said a second time. "I don't mind. It's not that far. My car's parked across the street. We might as well go right now." Mattie stood up and took her keys out of her purse. She would drive them to the airport. She wouldn't have to be by herself. "Well, let's go."

"Why, you can't do that," Bea said.

"Sure I can," Mattie said. In fact, she thought, I have to. I'm all alone in Palmer, don't know a soul; I just had two beers, for all I know I may be drunk. I can't drive home tonight. The distance is too great, and even if I could, Dad won't be waking up until morning, and Mother won't be waking up at all.

Nothing would have been too much. She would have driven these two women anywhere. She needed not to be alone. If she could attach herself to their lives, even for the afternoon, then she could leave her life here, come back to pick it up later on. She was sure it wasn't going anywhere.

"We don't even know your name," Bea said. Mattie knew that meant yes.

"I'm Mattie. Mattie Welsh. Let's go then."

"There's no rush," Babette said. "We have a little time." Now that it was settled, Babette took her beer and walked around the counter. "It's real nice of you to do this. Let me show you what I bought."

She was offering a treat. It was a ritual Mattie knew by heart, but one as puzzling to her as the Catholic hands grazing forehead, chest, shoulder, shoulder. A hundred times, Mattie had stood by while her sister Nancy unwrapped articles of clothing, skirts and blouses, dresses, shoes and coats, and said, "Look what I bought." Mattie's friend, Joanne, an artist who was working on a series of large oils entitled "Mothers in

Distress," said shopping was the only art some women had. It was the closest they came to creating anything. They were proud of their shopping, proud of the color and the fabric and the price—no matter high or low—proud as someone would be who had created something out of nothing, made a painting or a story or a song. "Look what I bought."

It was an idea that appealed to Mattie, made her feel tastefully superior. "I don't shop," she said in the same voice people use to say "We don't have a television."

Mattie's sister, Nancy, in a rare moment of confidence had told Mattie that her greatest fear about getting old was that she would lose her love of shopping, that she would be left at the end of her life with nothing to be interested in.

Whenever Mattie would visit her parents, Nancy and her mother would say with some genuine feeling, "Mattie, it would be so nice if you could get yourself something nice to wear."

For Mattie's part, she wished she could own seven outfits all the same, nondescript and comfortable, overlarge and not confining, which she would wear everywhere, and never have to think of what to wear again. As it was, Mattie frequently bought duplicates of turtlenecks and pullovers and denim skirts. She liked not to have to consider what to wear, and on those rare occasions when it seemed appropriate to try, she almost always guessed wrong, brought out something outdated, of a fabric or a pattern she had always liked; much as you take some friend out for Sunday drives because she's old and doesn't get out much.

Mattie's mother and her sister could have entire conversations about clothing. Mattie never paid attention; she could never figure out a way of joining in. She knew they both felt sorry for her and her wardrobe, and she purposely wore the same black-and-turquoise shirt for several summers in a row, when she went home to visit.

Babette had laid out on the counter two pink blouses, one plain, one with oversize roses, and a long black skirt.

"I can wear either of these blouses with the skirt," Babette said.

"Well, aren't you clever," Mattie said. Why was she so angry at this woman she didn't even know?

No matter. It had been the correct response. Babette beamed.

"Well, they're both beauties," Bea said. "No question. I always did say no one could shop like Babette. But I think we'd best be on our way. We don't want to hold this lady up if she's so nice to drive us."

Mattie left the bar with Bea and Babette, both of whom had dawdled, finding ten excuses to postpone departure: forgetting purse or scarf, needing drinks of water, one last, unnecessary trip to the bathroom, each, the two of them like children at bedtime, stalling well beyond the limits of anybody's patience.

"Let me just run these bags over to my car. Won't take a sec." Babette sped off down the sidewalk, just avoiding tripping in her silly heels.

"Damn," Bea said. "The security switch. Joe'll have my pension if I forget it one more time. 'What 'ya think I paid two thousand dollars for,' he'll say, and you don't want to see Joe disturbed. You just wait right here." Bea disappeared back inside.

Mattie had half a mind to leave the two of them, go pick up Jeannie at the airport, and be back before either of them had found another reason to delay. She walked over and plopped down on a green bench. The sidewalks were deserted. Where was everyone? At work. At home. Where Mattie should be. Mattie sat transfixed, her limbs limp and heavy. She wasn't sure that they would ever move again.

An old woman crab-walked into Mattie's line of vision, then froze there in the frame. She stood stock-still in the middle of the sidewalk, studying the opening and the closing hours on a sign posted on the door of the dry cleaners.

Well, Mattie thought, you have my full attention. Now what? Mattie was feeling the beer. At first, beer relaxed Mattie, made her feel contented, as though there might be several reasons to feel cheerful. But an hour or two later she always felt irritable, irritated. (Paul said, irritating.)

She stared at the old woman who seemed as though she might now stand planted there forever, refusing Mattie's strongest willing her away. The woman looked crazed, dazzled by the light, intent on some idea inside her head or maybe on an old thought, not remembered anymore but carried in some other way.

The woman was so old. Was it possible she ever had been young? It didn't seem likely. Mattie envisioned a little girl with sausage curls, dressed all in white and kelly green, with black high-button shoes, rolling a tall hoop. The woman rooted before her on the sidewalk never was that child. It was not possible. You could inquire of this old woman's mother; she would tell you certainly that this was not her little girl at all. A parent knows these things.

Mattie moved her tongue across her top front teeth and stared at the old woman.

What stands between you and me? she thought. What separates us? Maybe forty-five fast years, a few teeth, a certain pliancy of skin, already showing signs of wear, twenty truckloads of junk mail, sex a few hundred times, and each time with an older body. Forty Junes. Forty Februarys.

What separates me from you? Mattie said to the old woman no longer standing on the sidewalk, to the old woman who had at last remembered to be on her way. Only a dogged succession of days, pints of pancake makeup, quarts of ketchup, some grandchildren, and a lot of luck. Good luck. Excellent luck. Years together of near misses. Planes that touch down on both wheels; pulleys, cables, ropes that hold, traffic lights that function. Killers who strike someplace else, somebody else. Despair that never gets to totally despairing. Bridges kept in good repair, an immune system that doesn't give out, the good will and responsible behavior of a lot of strangers, even when they're tired.

Mattie turned her head, looked up and down the street, between the busy housewife-mother types with a reluctant child or two in tow, the teenagers, and the men in blue jeans, who all of a sudden were moving here and there, making the street not empty anymore. The old woman was gone, vanished, no sign of her. Mattie felt affronted. (She should not have had the second beer.) People wander in and out of your experience, occupy your thoughts at will, and disappear without a by-your-leave. Everyone who happens across your path is a potential deserter. Friends, your own children, people you have known, have been known by, all your life, can split at any moment, take a job and move away, send Christmas cards or not, or stay in town and get busy, lose interest or at least misplace it, stop calling and avoid you in the supermarket, rush by you on the street, calling over their shoulder that they're late for an appointment in another town. People can die on you.

Bea and Babette reappeared at the same moment. Mattie felt glad to see them.

"Come on, you two. Jeannie's plane is halfway to Harrisburg by now."

Mattie managed them across the street.

"Is this your car?" Bea's intonation said she hoped not.

"Yes, it is. Get in. It's just like a Chevy, only squarer, and safe to ride in."

"I've been in a Volvo before," Babette said, but she and Bea shared one expression.

"There, you see," Mattie said. "Go ahead, get in. It's not locked."

"I knew that," Babette said.

Babette settled her skirt with elaborate care and leaned forward to the radio. She smiled at Mattie. "What kind of music do you like?"

"Sixties. Early seventies. Would you put your seat belt on?" Mattie said. My mother died this morning in a car crash because she didn't have her seat belt on, she didn't say. "Bea, have you got your seat belt on back there?"

Mattie felt as though they were setting off for California, with plans to drive straight through. Bea and Babette spoke to one another as though Mattie weren't there, but clearly making conversation for her benefit. Mattie couldn't focus on their words, couldn't latch on to the subject. She was feeling fuzzy and not regular in any way.

What if she were to say to Bea and Babette, "Out. Get out, now. Go." She could put them out beside the road. It was no more than they deserved. They were both silly women, or at least Babette was.

Mattie picked up the signs for Route 80 East to Harrisburg and made her turn. She couldn't put them out. She had no one to replace them with. At least for the time being they were it.

It was not exactly without precedent: being stuck somewhere in between, needing help from someone, and at the same time wishing you didn't know them; being stuck with someone because you couldn't make it on your own.

Mattie clutched whenever it occurred to her that she might one day be in a position of needing help from her sister, Nancy. That was the way you always heard about it turning out. The tough independent one, the isolate, the one who left and moved away—only coming back for visits and not often— the black sheep, the rejected one, the Miss Superiority, that one, got sick, very sick, and was thrown back upon the mercy of the family. Who else? Who else can you really count on, they would say.

Mattie knew that Nancy would be spiteful enough to rise to the occasion, to visit Mattie in the hospital, at the extended care facility. Nancy would not, no, she most certainly could not, take Mattie in, she would tell her husband, late at night standing in the kitchen, sighing deep sighs, definite decided sighs, but she would visit Mattie every day, bringing women's magazines and a frilly pastel bed jacket with puffy sleeves.

"You want to look presentable," she would say.

"And about time," Mattie would sing back, and Nancy would purse her lips and sigh again, and say, "I didn't say that, Mattie. You did," and look long-suffering.

Nancy would stay each day for ten or fifteen minutes, until the conversation hit a major snag. She would stay until she had said, at least one time, "I know you won't like to hear this, Mattie, but..." She would stay until she had twice answered Mattie with her silence: her malicious, her I-told-you-so, her critical, and most of all, her unforgiving silence. The silence

Nancy could maintain for hours when they were growing up, for days stretched into months when they were older.

Silences and conversations. Mattie was hard pressed to say which one could hurt you more.

Her sister Nancy called, and after she hung up Mattie talked to her for hours. There are lots of conversations that don't end when the talking stops. They go on in your head, spin out, thin by the tail end of the afternoon, then pick up frenzy at the arsenic hour, in that interval between the failing light and evening—evening, now there's a word you wish would do just that. In your dreams, you write down smart rejoinders and your husband tells you in the morning you were snarling in your sleep.

Old, sister conversations with a half-life of twenty years. People say they take you back, back to family, as though family were some place or thing that could be left and then returned to. Family is not left luggage. Family is the baggage you drag with you everywhere. You might park it in the kitchen while you run upstairs to grab the laundry, but the beat-up pullman—that old brown herringbone, patterned with two stripes, one red, one green—that worn baggage trips you on the stairs.

And for all that, hope survives. A few months go by with little or no contact and you start to get ideas. The inspiration hits to take the family that you're carrying around with you to meet their forebears, take the replicas, the duplications and distortions, home to visit the originals. A meeting of the minds. A family reunion: like taking your idea of a vacation with you to some island you can get to on a special fare on the shirttails of high season.

A vacation. That's it. You wonder that you didn't think of it years ago. You will engineer a meeting of your brothers and your sister and your parents and the single aunt you shared among yourselves, at the beach. Not any beach. The beach where you went as children several summers in a row. What have you been thinking of? All those years returning to the scene of the crime, your childhood home, for every visit. It seems so misguided, so careless, looked at from this view. For all anybody knew, the whole family has been missing out on years of summer interludes on long, clean sandy beaches, on waves in temperate waters you could ride on sea sleds, or on inner tubes, or on your belly, over and again, until you raced back to the blanket for ice-cold lemonade in paper cups, and conversation, jokes, and nice remember-whens. Your kids would love it.

As it happens it will be your sister, Nancy, who refuses to go, refuses to meet the blanketfuls of relatives at Ocean Beach. ("Wasting her vacation time" is what she will claim to have no interest in.) And your brother David writes to say that he intends to be very busy (out straight? straight out?) for the whole summer, and Eddie does not write back either way, although on the telephone he said, Great idea. And then your mother writes to say she's very sure that all the children and their children would be happier at her house than at Ocean Beach. "Then everyone could feel relaxed," she writes, when you can summon up no conscious recollection of your own or anyone else's relaxation in that house in forty years.

Then, just like that, she up and dies. In an afternoon, your mother's gone, and with her any number of unlikely, outside possibilities, who knows how many might-have-beens. She's lost, vanished like the carved teak queen from the chess set in the den, and so from now on you will play without her, and always be surprised to think how many different ways she moved, how frequently she figured in your game.

HARRISBURG 37 MILES. Mattie wished it were farther. Bea and Babette had settled down into themselves, into their thoughts—if they did think—like two infants calmed by the vibration of the engine, the repeating rhythm of the road. The car felt peaceful now and self-contained; they weren't in need of anything from the outside. They could drive forever.

Mattie tried to think of when she had eaten something, but she couldn't pull it out. She had had the beer. She was almost certain beer had some food value. Brewer's yeast. People took it as a supplement; it was good for nursing mothers. Protein, she was almost sure.

Coffee. The one thing Mattie could have done with was a cup of coffee. Mattie, never certain if she craved the flavor and the welcome caffeine jolt, or the idea of the thing. Coffee steaming with associations of comfort and good will. Mattie loved the coffee commercials on TV, had her favorites. In one, a woman speaks with a voice from Texas in the 1930s, "It looks like it's gonna' be a nice day for the parade," and she pours coffee from a full round urn for everybody seated at the restaurant counter, and then they cut to scenes of a military parade, all shot in a grainy sepia. Mattie could watch this commercial a hundred times and never tire of it. She, who had never been to Texas nor would likely go, and who hated anything the least bit military.

Another favorite: a sheepish-looking young man is groping around a farmhouse kitchen at dawn trying to make coffee (decaf, which seemed to Mattie an exercise in futility, at 5 A.M.). Then you see his father and grandfather getting out of bed, and his mother rolling over and smiling (Mattie guessed because all the menfolk are hitting the fields and the woman knows she's free till lunch and thinks she might just grab another forty winks). The three generations of men leave the house in such a way to make you think that life is fundamentally a positive experience, that all things are possible to the farmer who gets up early, that hard work in the fields in the blazing sun gives you a charge, and that if you're having second thoughts about getting on with your life, a cup of Folgers, or maybe it was Maxwell House, will set you straight.

Mattie loved these commercials, and the ones for long-distance phone service and how it helps you stay in touch; only they never made her want a cup of coffee, any brand, or made her want to call anyone. They just made her feel she knew these people and the coffee shop on the parade route, and the farmhouse and the fields, and made her wish that she could go and live there and have coffee and watch the parade and plant and plow with them.

Mattie and her mother were the only members of the family who drank coffee. Nancy never did.

"Oh. Shit," Mattie said.

"What?" Bea was up at full attention.

"Nothing," Mattie said.

"Oh." Bea slumped back. Not even curious.

Shit, shit, shit, Mattie thought. She would have to go through all the funeral arrangements with Nancy, do the ghoulish shopping: mahogany or steel? concrete or wood? watertight or not? Her brothers, David and Eddie, were not even likely to be buffers, could not even be relied upon to join the fray. It was as though they had slept through certain years of their shared history, or been off somewhere playing ball. In family fights, either one of them could easily lose track of who the good guys and the bad guys were, could get distracted and go out to the kitchen to make a turkey sandwich. It was as though they had grown up in another room, or out in the backyard. It was like they didn't get it.

Mattie was always surprised when someone spoke about a sibling casually, mentioning a brother's job, or car, or heavy beard, saying, my sister has a chair—or a loveseat or a set of twins—just like that, or maybe talking about camping trips or Christmases they planned to spend together. Mattie hardly knew her brothers, always felt a little pretentious when she used the word. Mattie's brothers were years younger and had had a different mother, an older and more seasoned version, who, if she was not particularly fond of girls, liked boys a lot, and said so often and out loud. Nancy was closer to Mattie in age, but the two sisters had always been too caught up in surviving to notice one another much, unless they were competing for supplies. So Mattie and Nancy were strangers, in a complicated, tangled way, and they were enemies. Mattie's brothers were just strangers.

Now Nancy would be obsessed with what they dressed their mother in, with the cosmetics, and the styling of her hair. Nancy's voice, awash in platitudes, "Mother would have wanted..." Mattie screaming in her head.

The fallout. The repercussions. All the changes from one death. No change ever shows up alone. They go around in packs, and the whole lot of them stand out in the front yard while the first change, usually the biggest one, the fattest, the one with horns and face paint or a mask, comes knocking at your door. And you say, "Who's there?" or you run up the stairs and crawl on your belly underneath your bed. No matter, either way, by then the big change is in your living room and out on the back porch, and worrying the ceiling fan. And you, and all your relatives and friends and neighbors, are so taken with the big change—say, an earthquake or a plague. No, make it bigger than that. Say it is the death of one old woman—everyone's so busy noticing, and saying it's a lie, so taken up with feeding all the relatives who fly in from a thousand miles away with their four children, one with an infected eardrum, which could have easily ruptured on the airplane, but it didn't; everyone's so caught up dancing around the idea of the big change—go ahead, say it, death—that no one thinks to bolt the front door, tack up plywood on the windows, seal the chimney off, so that all the other changes are inside the house in the first fifteen minutes. "Why wait outside?" the long-range changes figure. "Let's go in. The moving van won't be here for eighteen months."

And so now the first change is filling up unlikely sections of the Pennsylvania turnpike, also parts of highways in Massachusetts and Ohio and New York. The big change, the bully, the show-off, is setting up religious services and getting written up in stilted language in three different small-town papers.

As for the rest, who will not show their faces for a year or ten years after that, they are all cowards, every blessed one. If Mattie weren't driving, she would get a piece of paper out and take down all their names.

Some had quaint, old-fashioned names no optimistic mother would consider: Sorrow and Regret and Grief and Mourning—which might better have been named to sound like night. Some had nicknames, like the Willies and the Heebee-Jeebies and the Blues, and some had scientific names, medical and psychiatric, and not even interesting to try to spell. Some names were French, like Pique and Ennui, and some sounded more like Chippewa or Mohawk or Shoshone: Burns-the-Rice, Moves-in-with-His-Daughter, Dances-with-Disaster, Plays-with-Fire, Sits-and-Stares, and some were cute soap-opera names like Remarriage, Florida, Fifty-Eight-Year-Old Stepdaughters, Legal Hassles.

But these were all just names for changes that would come to be. What about the names for things you get a written guarantee you won't be having now, the certain negatives: the dreary nursing home you will not set foot inside because your mother won't be there, the flannel nightgown lined in silk and decorated with a ribbon made of periwinkle blue that you won't be wrapping up on Mother's Day, the boring family picnics at the park you won't be eating now, the distant grand-mother your next son won't be having, the old and sudden disapprovals gone forever. No one ever now will be displeased with Mattie quite so much again.

But who knew? Who could say? The changes cooling their heels this moment in the front room at 311 Franklin Avenue might be the spoilers of the good, the wreckers of family happiness. If the first change had gotten the wrong address, or the right house one street over, if Mattie's mother had lived another ten or twenty years, they might have shared a pleasant conversation, more than one, several, one a day. Mattie and her mother might have bundled up in winter-time, and gone together for long walks, every afternoon at four o'clock—forget that Mattie lived, and not entirely by coincidence, five hundred miles away; forget they had not walked once together, not a step in forty years. They might have walked together in the failing light, and told each other stories of when they were small. Mattie would hear all about the little girl her mother was, and Mattie would tell her mother the story of when she was a little girl herself, and her mother would listen carefully, and when Mattie was all done, would say, "Well, I never *knew* that."

Mattie's mother might have lived to grow old, to ninety, or one hundred, and with extreme old age been whittled down, condensed, compressed, reduced to size, until all that was left would be a little old lady, no different really from someone who had been pleasant all her life, even to her family. She might have come to live with Paul and Mattie, baked frequent rhubarb pies, darned old socks, and been indiscriminately kind. Maybe that was all we needed, Mattie thought, just more time. Maybe the first fifty years of any relationship were always the hardest.

Or her mother might have lived only a few more hours, just till Mattie had arrived, just long enough to pull off one quick miracle, to whisper with her dying breath a phrase that would have leveled the playing field of Mattie's life, to speak softly in Mattie's ear, but loud enough so Nancy couldn't miss it, "Mattie, dear, I have been loving you forever. You turned out just the way I would have wanted me to be." Or, one better: "Mattie, my precious, precious girl, I always liked you best. You always were my favorite." And with that said, Mattie could have shared the planet with her sister for another forty years and never blinked, not one time, never again picked up the nail scissors to snip a family photograph in two: one piece Mattie and her mother and a thin sliver of Nancy's arm; one piece Nancy, with her amputated sweater, standing all alone.

The smallest thing could make the biggest difference. What if the whole thing were just some slight misunderstanding?

Like when you say *okay*, only the other person hears it as *go away*. Or when you tell someone you're sorry, only they don't hear you, because the water's running, or they've fallen asleep, or they've grown up and moved away. And if the error were so flimsy and so slight, then so should the remedy be, too. Like saying, "Oh, no, I didn't say die, I said hi." The fix so quick and easy, like standing something upright, that had been knocked over, forty years ago, by accident, and left to lie there all that time.

"I hope Jeannie's not all tired out. She always comes home so played out," Bea said. "She goes to bed right after supper when she's home and sleeps till noon. I don't think she sleeps in New York City. I don't imagine anybody does."

Mattie blinked, several times, on purpose.

"Well, if she goes to bed early, I won't see her much," Babette said. "I have to go over to Sunbury tomorrow with Tiffany. They've got their shoes on sale. You know the time I have finding shoes I like. I'd like to get a pair of red pumps, and a blue pair if I can find some. I don't know what time we'll get back."

"Maybe Jeannie'd like to go with you," Bea said without conviction.

"Do you work?" Mattie asked Babette, purposely omitting the politically correct, "outside the home," which always struck Mattie as more than just a little patronizing.

"Do I work? Do I ever. Four full days a week. At the Center of Life. I'm the director there."

Mattie hoped that Babette would not elaborate.

"Do you have children?" Mattie said.

"Do I have children? Two. A little girl and a boy, Todd James. Oh yes, I am a career woman and a mother. Most people wonder how I do it all. Sometimes I wonder myself." Babette leaned back against the headrest, apparently exhausted by the very thought.

Mattie looked in the rearview mirror. Bea was staring out the side window, not moving at all. She might be dead. How do you look when you're dead. Mattie could remember dead great-uncles lying in their tufted, pastel, satin-lined caskets, faces pink flesh-toned, and looking finer certainly than ever in real life when they always wore two sets of long underwear under a green work shirt bound with their maroon suspenders and a belt pulled very tight.

The shiny metal caskets. The solemn funerals. As a child, Mattie loved the day of any funeral, such a fine occasion for puzzling it all out, observing unobserved, imposing order on the entire allotment of relations and figuring just where she herself might fit in the assortment, and in the space of one long afternoon, laying in a store of attitudes and inclinations against whatever was to come.

Mattie could see them now. The rooms of relatives, the bereaved—relieved, or not—the blood relations, or the ones connected up some way by marriage. Fifty-year-old cousins riding in the fourth car, sighing heavy sighs. Women dressed in feather black, or navy, that looked good beneath the pearls. Tall men in lint-free black suits, backs pressed against the wind. (It was never warm when they were buried.) Silent, grave pall-bearers, Mattie could see them, standing still, each with his top hand gripping the one underneath, as though that were the only force holding everything together.

Then later, back at the house, the ladies from the church uncovering tables of aluminum-shrouded surprises, and the fat uncles, busy aunts, and the second cousins once-removed who came from out of town, but only for the day, stood eating fried chicken and ham and sweet potatoes baked with crusty marshmallows on top, each mourner seeming to himself appropriate, exactly suited. A funeral could make it all so orderly and dignified, with resolution, definition, absolute, at least for the remainder of the afternoon. Death used to keep fine company, had its own ceremonies, ancient rites, and holidays.

Holidays like Good Friday—a day about death if there ever was one. It had always been Mattie's favorite day of the whole year. Christmas and her birthday were set-up let-down days, but Good Friday delivered: drama, darkening skies and thunder rumbles, and every year, the same story, the one that broke God's heart.

When Mattie was a little girl, she went to church at noon on Good Friday with her mother and her brother and her sister and her aunt. They all wore their winter coats and sat three-quarters of the way back in the First Presbyterian Church where decorum was a virtue and restlessness and shuffling feet and chewing gum were cardinal sins right up there with pride and fornication. The whole town shut down from noon until three o'clock, the stores, the banks, the B. & B. Restaurant, the public library. No books would be checked in or out before the temple veil was rent in twain—the awe as everyday and practical as that. Mattie liked to think, even though she sat inside and never witnessed it firsthand, that every year the sky went black from noon till three o'clock, and there were noises coming from above the sky, like thunder, only higher up, or rumbling, from beneath the ground.

At three o'clock the stores and banks and library would open up and Mattie and her sister, and her mother and *her* sister would all go buy Easter hats. There were five hat shops in

Granby in those years, five hat shops, four five-and-tens, a hotel, and two each of movie theaters, drugstores, and men's and ladies' clothing stores.

One year Mattie bought a bright orange hat, a helmet shape with overzealous, pumpkin-colored roses all around. One year she got a yellow picture hat whose wide brim drooped and melted Easter morning, fell in dips around her face, until she had to lift one corner of the brim to peer out or answer back when anybody said hello.

After the hat shops, they went to Woolworth's or McCrory's to buy soft, pale, downy ducks, and yellow baby chicks. Peeps, they called them. They always died. Some didn't live till Easter morning. But alive, they peeped all night in newspaper-lined, high-sided boxes on the kitchen floor.

Something in Mattie loved thinking about all these things that weren't anymore, good and bad, people and marriages and hat shops and her old elementary school and baby chicks and her first mother-in-law. Mattie was attracted to the notion that a thing could be gone, finished and done with forever. Her first husband and his disposition and his whole complement of relatives, her ex-priest, the dentist she didn't go to anymore, her third-grade teacher, who could never hurt her again, or not in real life. Mattie liked these exes.

Xs. Like crossing out mistakes. It makes you feel that nothing is irrevocable, so long as you swear you didn't really mean it in the first place. Mattie had recently run into a girl named Bobbi, a girl she had gone to school with, a cheerleader who had been queen and president of everything. Mattie had spent four years of her life wanting to be Bobbi. She had on more than one occasion suffered gross embarrassment when she had a chance to speak with Bobbi face to face. But the middle-aged prom queen didn't remember Mattie at all, and Mattie had been entirely happy with Bobbi's frank bewilderment. Not being remembered can be refreshing. It feels for all the world like absolution, forgiveness, total and sincere. If they don't remember who you are, they are unlikely to recall your sins, your awkward, gawky, adolescent failings. So all you are responsible for is you for this five minutes. Nobody's asking you to bear the weight of your whole life. It's the best kind of blank slate there could be.

A blank slate, wiped clean, with everything and everybody you regretted all exed out. Mattie liked the fresh startness of the thing, and yes, she liked the hanging on, the refusal to let go of the little threads and snippets of her choosing. She went back time and again to visit hat shops in Granby that had closed down years ago. She browsed and idly tried on hats and asked the woman in the purple flowered dress to tell her did she think the shiny cherry baubles were too busy with her glasses, the bright green silk leaves too summery for this late in the year.

Mattie looked down at the clock on the dashboard. It said ten o'clock. She reset it to 4:15 to match her watch. Mattie wished she could set everything right this way. Whenever someone died, it felt like God was giving you another chance, but not without first calling it to your attention just how far off course you might have drifted. Mattie did not subscribe to magazines that called God subtle. Not with original inventions like death and resurrection, not with a day like Good Friday on the calendar every blessed year.

"Oooouuuuuuuhhhhh," Bea breathed out a strange sound from the backseat.

"Bea, are you awake back there?" Mattie said. Are you alive

back there? Mattie used the voice that people use with children and with people who are very old.

"I'm awake," Bea said. "Just dozing." As though sleep and wakefulness were the same thing.

"Jeannie'll probably be all wrinkled when we pick her up." Babette's eyes had fluttered open. Mattie saw her blinking several times as if to readjust to twenty-twenty. "You have no idea what she'll have on. You never know what to expect with Jeannie. She might show up, even traveling by plane, in some old skirt and the turtleneck she bought over at the P.T. the time she shopped with us because they were having a going-out-of-business sale. The only way she'll buy clothes is if they're ninety percent off, and then she won't care if a thing comes in her size, or even in her color. She'll buy anything if the price is low enough, buy something no one else would carry off for free. You wanna' stick of gum?"

Mattie shook her head.

"Mum, gum?" Babette held out a pack of Juicy Fruit to Bea, and Mattie caught a whiff. She would have liked to take a stick to hold and sniff and to remember with.

"Can't," Bea said. "Sticks to my partial. You got any mints? My mouth is that dry." Bea's voice sounded like she had just come back from far away, from someplace where she hadn't had to use her voice.

Babette fished out a white Canada mint, which Mattie would have liked to hold in her other hand, and sniff, alternating with the Juicy Fruit.

"You wanna' mint?" Babette said.

Mattie was convinced Babette would not address her by her Christian name, if life depended on it. She would hit Mattie over the head to get her attention, and then call her "you," or "she" in conversation.

"No, Babette. Thank you."

"Now, what were we discussing?" Babette said. "Oh yes. What Jeannie is likely to show up in. Don't be shocked if you see her in a nice blouse or a pullover top that looks new, and then some weird kind of skirt, like a cotton wrap-around, or one with shoulder straps, and then knee socks and black running shoes. I don't know if she doesn't know any better, or if she just doesn't care what people think." Babette took a bottle of nail polish from her purse, and opened it, obliterating any memory of Juicy Fruit or peppermint. "I hope you don't mind."

Mattie shrugged. She calculated Babette would need to give her full attention to her nails.

What people think. The words ringing back. The idea filling the whole car like the noxious scent of lacquer. What people think.

When Mattie was a little girl, whole conversations had been given over to what-people-think. You bought clothing, passed comment, got pregnant, chose your house paint and your husband, your seat, your attitudes, your means of traveling from one place to another, accordingly. In Mattie's family, what-people-think passed for religion, competing in an overcrowded field. And more remarkable than that, what-people-think was generally understood, a matter of unspoken consensus.

"What will people think?" Words never spoken by a man. Oh no, it would be Mattie's mother, or an aunt, or grandmother who would intone the litany, entirely confident the answers would be obvious, even to little Mattie.

AIRPORT   6 MILES

Mattie took the turnoff. Uncle Bing came uninvited to her mind. Uncle Bing, a blood relative, a tangent in the mainstream of relations, and for all that, a man who did not know what people think, did not appear to give consideration to the matter. He was perhaps the only member of Mattie's family who did not in some way embarrass her.

Uncle Bing, Arthur Albert to his mother at his birth and still at the age of sixty-five when she said it for the final time, just plain Arthur to the preacher, and to the young intern who treated Uncle Bing with Gelusil and Maalox for cancer of the colon, and then later with surgery and radiation and two different kinds of chemotherapy, when it was a silly thing to do to anyone who at the age of eighty-seven had never been inside a hospital, not even as a restless visitor; to anyone who had no health insurance, because he hadn't worked in fifty years, had not signed up for Medicare—hadn't heard he needed to, or thought the letter in the mail that said he should did not apply to him. He came from people who paid cash, and he did pay, more than fifty thousand dollars—all of his life savings that there was to talk about.

That's not counting the house his mother left him down on Brady Street, the gray three-story, with fire-engine-red, Benjamin Moore Satin Gloss trim on alternating windows, and bright electric blue on all the other windows in the front. Around the back, the window trim was several different colors, clearly the tail-end of many cans, purchased in the first place for what purpose Mattie could not imagine; many cans, some mixed, some applied straight, not mixed, not even stirred up properly, so that the color deepened, was more true, as it progressed toward the top of the window frame or down the other side. But the window trim attracted little notice after the first time, the trim a silent backdrop for a whole backyard full of painted wheels: bicycle wheels, glossed-over red and pink and brown and green and yellow; thirty or maybe forty wheels, each mounted on a metal pole, upright at full attention, holding up a wheel; the entire backyard, except for the cucumbers and the lettuces and drooping fat tomato plants, the whole yard, taken over by the wheels which, at this moment, Mattie wasn't certain moved round with the wind, or held firm, no matter what the weather. These were wheels that anyone—a senile woman with her mind in permanent suspension, or a boy who was and always would be in some kind of trouble with the police, or a stranger driving through, or even a religious person—wheels that anyone could wonder at or be surprised about, and notice every single time he walked by, even if he lived next door.

"It's different if you have to live in the same town with Uncle Bing," Mattie's sister, Nancy, said, and sighed.

But Mattie never was embarrassed, never had been, by the wheels or by the window trim or by the green long underwear her uncle wore even in hot weather, or by the roomers—rumors, Mattie had thought when she was very young—the single men who rented single rooms and lived for decades there—and for certain, not embarrassed by the miniature woman, Lily, with the bright blue eyes in a face still pretty at age ninety, who slept on a tiny cot in the corner of Bing's bedroom for the last eight or ten years of her life. Bing said Lily was afraid to sleep in a room by herself, and besides, there was plenty of floor space.

It made sense. Lots of people fall off to sleep more easily in company. It's only when you are awake you sometimes feel the need to be alone, and then you can choose the time. But in the hours of the night, it seemed right there should be somebody there in the next bed; then, if you sleep or not, you know that it's okay.

Mattie had always respected Uncle Bing. You will respect a person who does not think himself about what other people think.

Babette finished polishing her last fingernail, and screwed the bottle closed with just her palm and thumb.

"There," Babette said. "Now I'm ready for old Jeannie."

CHAPTER EIGHT

MATTIE CAUGHT HER breath and made a little coughing noise, only breathing in, not out—a cough heading in the wrong direction. It reminded Mattie of a child's whistle, if you put it in your mouth and inhale. Neither Bea nor Babette said anything. They didn't notice. Or they didn't care. Mattie inhaled again. She thought she heard the raspy noise, but she wasn't sure. Maybe she was having an asthma attack. She didn't have asthma, but she had been on the lookout for years. It seemed like one of the scariest things you could have and not die from, one of the most frightening things you could live with, never knowing when would be the next time you couldn't breathe.

Mattie coughed out loud. A made-up cough, like when the

doctor wants to listen to your lungs and says, "Cough, please," without saying how. The cough sounded normal enough. She breathed deeply through her nostrils, then with her mouth wide open.

"Are you okay?" Babette seemed to regain consciousness at will. She cracked her gum. "You okay?"

"What do you mean?" Mattie hated it when people asked if you were okay, because they only seemed to ask when you weren't sure.

"Well, you were breathing funny. You a smoker?"

"No, I'm not a smoker," Mattie said.

"You don't look that good." Babette leaned forward and turned at a peculiar angle which made it hard for Mattie to concentrate on the road.

"I'm fine. I'm tired. I had two beers. I never have two beers."

"Beer won't hurt you. Beer's good for you, helps you relax. Maybe you need to relax more. They're saying now that stress is bad for you."

"What airline is your sister flying?" Mattie's anger at Babette was making her feel better. She tried one long slow breath. It sounded perfectly regular. She was in a very low risk group for an early heart attack.

"Allegheny," Bea said. "Jeannie always travels with the Allegheny Airlines."

"US Air, Mum. They changed the name years ago," Babette said to her mother.

"US Air," Babette repeated the words as though Mattie could only hear when she was addressed directly.

"It's still a very good airline service." Bea was such a different person since she had gotten in the car, as though even the idea of Jeannie required new behavior.

Mattie thought the car sounded funny. She wasn't sure if it was the tires or the road, but there was a lump-lump sound that was new. She concentrated on the evenly spaced seams of tar across the highway. Their timing corresponded with the noise. Well. That was all right then. But something was wrong, and she couldn't tell if it was her body or the car, or something else.

"I lied to you." Mattie heard herself speaking in a stagy voice. "My mother didn't die a few years ago. She died this afternoon. Just before I came into the bar." Her voice sounded odd, as though there were an echo in the car.

"What?" Babette said.

"I'm not talking to you," Mattie said. "I'm talking to your mother. You drive a person crazy. Did it ever occur to you that I might be speaking to your mother, that every word that's said is not expressly for your ears?"

"Well. Excuse me." Babette sounded pleased. She adjusted her skirt, smoothed back her hair, then went looking through her purse, pulling out a roll of mints and making an elaborate production of disposing of her gum.

"Bea. Did you hear what I said?" Mattie wondered how Bea could stand Babette.

"Why, yes I did. I was just taken aback there for a minute. I'm not sure I exactly understand," Bea said.

"My mother died today. She's only been dead about five hours. She was totally alive this morning. She was at least partially alive till after twelve o'clock. Yesterday she probably went to the supermarket and talked to people that she hardly even knew about the cantaloupes and her new coat and the cold weather. She probably didn't sleep too well last night—she never does, hasn't for years. She and my father probably didn't say much to each other this morning. I bet they had breakfast at entirely different times, ate completely different things, and she probably thought that tonight she'd wash her hair and finish with the ironing, so the ironing board is probably still standing, set up in the dining room, a skirt she ironed and decided at the last minute not to wear still lying across the ironing board."

Mattie was shaking all over, and her teeth were making a clicking noise that sounded mechanical and too fast to Mattie's ears.

"Well, now," Bea said. "Well, now."

"Pull over here," Babette said. "There's a cutout up ahead. I'll drive."

Mattie did as she was told but stopped the car too abruptly, jolting the three of them.

"Now, get out a minute," Babette said.

Mattie opened her door and swung her legs around, her feet reaching for the pavement which seemed strangely far away. She felt like she was just coming home from the hospital the same day she had surgery on her stomach.

"Now get out, and walk up and down the road a ways," Babette said. "Move real brisk. Walk hard."

Mattie got out of the car as though she were disabled. She stood stiffly and walked with obvious attention to her feet. She looked aimless as she moved away from the car.

"Babette, she's gonna' get herself killed. She'll walk into the traffic. Call her back here. The cars can't see her."

"No, Mum. Believe me. She needs a few minutes to get herself back together. Get her blood pumping. She's probably been sitting too long."

"But she said her mother just died."

"I heard her."

"Well, what do you make of that?" Bea saw Mattie walking farther into the distance. It looked like she was moving with some speed.

"Go after her, Babsie."

"No. She needs this."

"Well, what are we gonna' tell her when she gets back. If she comes back at all. She might just keep on goin'. How come she was drivin' us to Harrisburg in the first place with her mother lyin' dead. You can't figure out some people."

"She's in shock. You read about people being in shock. They do strange things. I hope this car drives like a regular car. There. She's turning back. See, I told you."

"Well, what are we to say to her?"

"Just act natural. She'll probably be still in shock."

"Why isn't she going to her mother?"

"Her mother's dead."

"Yes, well, you know what I mean. Maybe we should take her to a hospital."

"It's not that kind of shock."

Mattie came within range of the car, then spun around in the direction she had come. She moved off as though she had some destination.

"You go get her now, Babette, and we'll get Jeannie. Maybe Jeannie can give her some pills or something."

"Mum, we don't need Jeannie. We're handling this just fine. You can see she's walking straighter."

"I hate to say it, but I'm afraid we'll be late."

"Well, it won't kill Jeannie to wait."

Mattie's face appeared at the side window.

"Get in." Babette's voice was even.

"I'm very hungry, shaky hungry." Mattie got in. "I think I need to eat now."

"We'll get you some supper at the airport," Bea said.

"No," Mattie said. "I have food here."

"Well, there you go." Babette moved the car slowly down the shoulder of the road, both hands gripping the steering wheel near the top. "We'll just drive right along then."

Mattie broke off a chunk of Cheddar cheese and folded a slice of bread around it. The taste was wonderful. She took several bites, then opened a box of apple juice and took a long slow drink, emptying a fair amount of the container. It was the best apple juice she had ever tasted.

"I'm sorry I snapped at you." She turned to Babette, who was fully focused on the road. "I'm always crabby when I'm hungry. Anyone in my family could tell you that."

"Well, don't you worry about it," Bea said. Babette gave no evidence of having heard. "No. You just don't even think of it. You just eat. You just take your time."

Babette took the size of the steering wheel and its position as specifically intended personal affronts. But the more she grumbled, the better Mattie felt. She polished off the rest of the cheese and bread, and started on the bag of Fig Newtons. Mattie could remember that food had tasted this good after the birth of her two children. Ravenous, she had gulped glasses of ginger ale and cranberry juice, and hours later, sitting sideways on the bed, legs dangling across cold metal bars—an infant, hours old, away somewhere—she had savored boiled potatoes, amazing meatloaf, applesauce, and spongy beige bread with real butter, then Salada tea. "Beauty is as beauty does," the tea tag read the day Andy was born.

At one point, it seemed to Mattie, Babette was inclined to

ditch the car and continue to the airport on foot, but in the end, she managed to negotiate the vicissitudes of airport routings, and if they ended up in long-term parking, they arrived in reasonably good shape.

"I've never driven a car like this before." Babette handed Mattie back the keys.

Mattie turned sideways in her seat. Bea was combing her hair with some force, and Babette took out a makeup kit, signaling a major overhaul: bottles, jars, and plastic squares revealing every color—not just pastels, but army green, a real fruit orange, clown white. Mattie nestled back. She loved to watch other people do things to their faces, make real changes. It made Mattie think that people weren't as stuck as you imagined.

"Babette, we'll be late for Jeannie." Bea took out a compact of her own, and a lipstick, an unfortunate shade and texture. She applied a heavy coating, then blotted her lips over and again until they looked like she had just finished eating something barbecued in sauce. Babette opened six or eight different plastic squares and used a sequence of separate brushes. Finally, Babette folded up her case. Mattie thought she looked more rested. Clearly, Babette knew her stuff. Mattie reached into the side compartment of her purse and pulled out a lipstick.

"I'm sorry"—Babette touched Mattie's arm—"but we really have to go now."

Inside the airport, the noise and the unnatural light made it feel like 3 A.M. Mattie and Babette and Bea walked the long padded corridor like three no-nonsense women leaving on a business trip. Mattie wondered what people did on business trips. Unless they were displaying samples of a product from a large black leather case, what business could not be conducted by telephone? But everyone in business always seemed to go there, in person. You saw them waiting at airports, with a newspaper or magazine—never with a paperback—sometimes with an open briefcase revealing two or three solid inches of white paper, all bound together or in stapled clumps. Once on the plane, they never read the safety instructions, or looked at the stewardess or out the window.

"There she is," Babette shrieked as though she hadn't actually expected Jeannie to show up.

"There she is," Bea said.

Mattie ticked off the faces as they moved not unselfconsciously along the narrow, roped-off corridor toward the clump of greeters, family members, or good friends. Mattie didn't see Jeannie.

"Hello, Mother. Babette." A slight woman touched Bea's arm and seemed to smile at Babette. Mattie scanned the crowd again. This must be Jeannie after all. She readied for the introductions.

"Why, Jeannie, could I have a word with you?" Bea took her daughter's arm and led her a few feet away toward the window.

"We have this girl here. Her mother just died somewhere else, and she's in shock," Bea said.

Mattie heard enough to get the gist. She stared at Babette, who looked like she was doing antiwrinkle exercises with her face.

"No. No, she drove us to the airport to pick you up," Mattie heard Bea hiss. Bea caught Mattie's eye and smiled and gave a little wave.

"I didn't mean for her to tell everybody," Mattie said to Babette.

"It's all right," Babette said. "Jeannie won't say anything. She hardly even pays attention when you tell her things in the first place, and even if she does hear you, she forgets."

Bea and Jeannie walked over. "Well, we can go," Bea said. "I wanted to make sure Jeannie didn't have any more suitcases to get."

"Hi." It seemed to Mattie that Jeannie was addressing her.

"Hi," Mattie said.

As though experiencing some delayed reaction, Bea and Babette greeted Jeannie as if she had just gotten off the plane.

"How was your flight? Was it bumpy? Did they feed you? Is that skirt new?"

Mattie led the way through the parking lot. She had the keys. Bea and Babette had fallen silent. Mattie turned the key in the door, unlocking all four doors. Bea and Babette climbed into the back. Jeannie hesitated and then got into the front seat.

Their hands grazed when Mattie and Jeannie fastened their seat belts in the center clasp, but neither spoke. If you don't speak to someone at the first, Mattie thought, like if the two of you are the only ones waiting in a line, then it becomes harder later on to talk. You conspire together at a silence of its own invention.

Mattie handed the pudgy woman in the parking lot booth three dollars. No one offered any contribution. Mattie suspected any one of them, alone, would have insisted upon paying; but put people together in a car with members of their family and each and every one of them will be the child.

Mattie took a right at the stop sign, drove up the feeder road to the main highway. There was a dead animal lying on the shoulder. Freshly dead. Recently deceased. Death has not just its euphemisms but exclusive rights to certain words and phrases.

Death, Mattie thought, not just funerals, but death. There's that to be considered now, to be walked cautiously around, examined from every angle, death to be thought about in all of its particulars.

Deaths of parents. Deaths of distant relatives. Deaths of strangers. Deaths of children. No, that one can't be thought about. Go back to deaths of strangers. Your wife's first fiancé, the deceased whose job your husband takes, the maiden lady, forty-seven, who dies in her sleep of natural causes—as though dying all alone, when you have just begun to get some rough idea of what it's all supposed to be about, were natural in any way—the maiden lady, forty-seven, whose house you buy and raise your children in, the house you live on in long after the divorce, long after they are grown and gone away. The deaths of strangers can have an impact on you every day, change where you shop for groceries, and how much you spend.

The deaths of parents. Mattie held her arms straight and taut from her shoulders to the steering wheel, leaning back as far as possible. Parents. You live always with the idea of their deaths, Mattie thought, however much you might think otherwise. Their deaths are real for you, for the first time, when you are six years old, and they refuse to promise you that they will never die. They won't promise—or they dance around it in a way that amounts to very much the same thing—no matter how hard you try to let them know it's not negotiable as far as you're concerned. So very early on you get the message that it's really just a matter of time. Tomorrow, or later on tonight, or fifty years from now, they're going to die. No matter if they lead you down the garden path on every other issue, on this one point they are inflexible. They intend to die. Hard pressed and pushed enough, they won't deny that you will, too, but that won't penetrate, or not with any terror, until you're nine or ten.

So from this early calculating on, forever after that, you will be making some accommodation to their dying, in your mind and in your planning. And the fact that they are still breathing in the middle of the night when you go in to tell a dream, and that they show up at your graduations and your weddings and your christenings and at the fortieth anniversary party which you give them in a restaurant, doesn't hold out any contradiction. It just removes, at each commemoration, one more of the hurdles they seem slated to clear before they go; and you and everybody else by then will say, they're not as young as they once were (i.e., they will be dying sooner now than later). And so, it's pretty clear that all along, for your whole life, or ever since you got the word, it's something you have been expecting.

Then, the topper is that everybody's always so surprised. The day it finally happens, or the next day, or two weeks after that, they say out loud to several people, "I just can't take it in," as though every time somebody dies, it feels like the first time, like something that never happened before—literally true for the deceased—as though death were reinvented every time another person dies. What was the vaudeville line? People are dying now who never died before.

"I don't know what some of these clerks think you're supposed to do." Mattie realized Babette had been speaking for some time. "I was in the dressing room with a size eight and I knew there was a ten out on the rack 'cause I'd seen it, and do you think the girl would go get it for me? I had to get dressed and go out for it myself."

"Who's with the kids?" Bea asked.

The two women traded words of little or no consequence, Mattie thought, even to themselves. Their words a buffer, some old guarantee that Jeannie would not attempt to break in. She seemed to Mattie not a major threat. Jeannie was ignoring them, or they were ignoring her. This is crazy, Mattie thought. I drove halfway across Pennsylvania to pick up this woman and bring her back to visit these two people she doesn't seem to want to pass the time of day with, and they're carrying on a conversation as though Jeannie weren't even there.

"So," Mattie said. "So, Jeannie, what brings you to Palmer?" Mattie was feeling prickly, all across her skin and inside as well.

"Why, she comes down to see us all," Babette said. "Wants to keep in touch with the home folks."

"Jeannie comes down every year this time," Bea said. "Mind the time it snowed? One of them freak storms. Snowed to beat the band and Jeannie had to stay on an extra day."

"I'm not sure I understand how it came about that you drove my mother and my sister to the airport." Jeannie's diction was precise.

"I told you," Bea said. "She came by the bar while I was working, and when she heard about Babette's car, why she said she'd bring us on over. It sure was nice of her. You have to admit that."

Apparently Jeannie didn't.

"Would you have any interest in going shoe shopping with me tomorrow, Jeannie?" Babette leaned forward, although her voice would have carried from the next car. "I have to tell you we'll be getting an early start, and we're making a day of it."

"She's all tired out, Babette." Bea sighed a long, tired sigh. "She doesn't want to be running all over creation the first day home."

"I'm going to need to stop for gas." Mattie realized she

needed to get outside and walk again. This wasn't working. Not at all. Ever since she had told Bea and Babette about her mother, she had the feeling she was moving around with a gaping hole in her, her stuffing coming out, in little bits and pieces, on the floorboard and the seat. She needed to hold her hand across the hole, to stuff it back inside; only it seemed the hole kept changing its location, and that her hands were floppy, rag-doll hands that were no good for holding anything. She had put masking tape where she thought the problem was; only it kept tearing loose and sticking to itself.

"I am in a peculiar situation." Mattie turned toward Jeannie speaking in a voice full enough to make her turn and look. "I know you know. My mother just died. I don't know what it's like for other people, but I think I might be losing my mind, and if you're a doctor, you probably did a psych rotation, so maybe you could talk me down. I'm sorry. I hate to do this. I know it puts people on the spot when you're too needy. But I'm feeling weird, strange. I ate something, but it didn't last. I've been driving all day. That'll do it to you. The motion thing. It makes you feel disoriented. Like, after you've been driving all day, and you stop to get a soda, and your legs feel funny when you walk across the parking lot. Your whole body feels like you're still riding in the car. Like when you first take off your roller skates. I used to roller skate in Palmer when I was eight. Every Friday night, like clockwork. It cost fifty cents. Thirty-five to skate and fifteen to rent the skates. I might have seen you there. I think we must be about the same age. My mother gave me the fifty cents on Friday nights to go, and one time when we had company from out of town—it must have been relatives because one of them gave me fifty cents—and after supper, I stood around on one foot waiting for my skating money but afraid to ask, and finally it got late, and so I asked my mother in her ear, and she laughed out loud, in front of a whole kitchen table full of relatives we hardly ever saw. She was sarcastic—that was her thing—and made me feel like an idiot, because I hadn't known that she expected me to use my present money to pay for skating. I felt like a fool. That's why I'm so screwed up with this. Those are the only kinds of things I can bring back. All petty little things that don't matter, that don't sound like anything to tell when I hear myself say them. It sounds funny when I talk about it, but it was my life, and I was so impressionable. Things never beaded, never rolled like water off my back, as they sometimes seem to do.

"Stupid stories. That's all that's there. I can remember only stupid little stories. Grievances. Things that put her in a bad light in my mind. I can't feel sad, or normal, or even surprised. I just feel like I'm falling into pieces, and I need to get stuck back together."

"I think she needs to walk again," Babette said.

"I swear to God. The three of you never say a word head-on to anyone. You answer for each other and everything you say about a person, it's like they aren't there." Mattie turned full around to face Babette.

"Why don't you let me drive," Jeannie said.

"I don't believe this family," Mattie said. "Every time I tell one of you my mother just died, you offer to drive."

"What would you like us to do?" Jeannie said.

Now, that's more like it. Mattie took hope. It came as a sort of jolt.

"Well," Mattie said, "I want you to talk to me about it; say what it's like for other people, tell me about the lady down the street when her dog got run over; circle round it, then close in;

tell me, Bea, what you felt when your mother died; make me see that what I'm going through today is normal in some way and that I'll get over it."

"Get over it," Babette said. "It seems to me that you're just now getting into it."

"To tell the truth, my mother's still alive," Bea said. A soft apology.

"Well, you know what I mean. Talk with me about it. Engage. Don't dance around it. Don't avoid it. I hate it when people pretend nothing's going on."

"Why don't you tell us about your mother." Babette leaned forward, pleased to have a plan. "At funeral parlors, people always say, 'Oh, yes, remember Joe, how he always did thus and so,' and everybody nods, and feels a little sad, and a little better."

"That's the worst idea you could have come up with." Mattie saw the sign for Route 80 almost too late, and made a sharp turn without warning to the driver behind her, who laid on his horn. "My mother is exactly what I can't talk about. You won't understand this. You and Bea seem so scrambled up with one another. But I never felt as though I knew my mother. We talked once or twice a year on the phone, and when I was growing up I don't remember her at all, and she was no place else but home with us kids. My father was the one who was always out somewhere, and I remember him in a million stories, on a million different days. My mother was there giving us our baths, or getting us dressed up for church, complaining all the while that my father never was around to help."

"See there," Babette said. "You came up with a memory of her, just like that. This is probably very good for you. Go on. Just remember."

Mattie thought it was like telling someone to sneeze.

"Do you remember me?" Bea's voice was small and sounded like she hadn't used it in a long time.

"Of course."

"Not really."

Jeannie and Babette said the words at the same time; actors poorly rehearsed. For a moment Mattie was confused about which daughter had voiced which answer.

"What do you remember?" Bea said. Her voice was flat and didn't rise to lift the question at the end.

"Oh, lots of stuff," Babette said.

"Hardly anything." Jeannie's words followed her sister's as though this time they had agreed upon the speaking order in advance.

"What do you mean?" Bea said a second time.

"Oh, I remember little dresses that you bought us," Babette said, "with smocking and sash ties and embroidery on the front, and a three-foot doll I got from Santa, and a Brownie camera you bought me when I was in the first grade, and lots of things."

"I can't remember much at all," Jeannie said. Her turn. "I've tried sometimes to sit down at a table and to make a list, but nothing comes. Oh, I mean I remember that you always asked the waitress for your coffee with your dinner, and I remember once you told me how amazed you were when you found out you were pregnant with me, and that you took a full Christmas dinner down to Uncle Simon on a plate every Christmas, and I remember how you always hated any shade of blue, but I do not remember that you ever played with me or ever really talked to me."

Mattie held her breath. Jeannie had just said the words that Mattie hadn't ever said, would not, now, ever have the chance to choose one day to say to her own mother. She wished she had a tape recorder running, could record the words Bea gave back in reply. Why? Were the words of all mothers interchangeable? Could one woman speak for them all?

Silence. Bea had no words to answer for herself, much less for Mattie's mother.

"Now Jeannie, I don't know how you can say that," Babette said. "Why, I remember Mum playing in the snow with Peter and Ralphie when they were little boys. And she used to take Ralphie up his breakfast in bed when he was in high school. He was playing football and he liked to eat right away when he woke up."

"Well, Jeannie," Bea said. "I remember you. I don't remember that you played with me, or talked with me much either, but Jeannie, I remember you."

"My mother would have said that, too," Mattie said. "She would have told you she remembered me, but what you'd hear about would be how she ironed the little dresses, and the fabric, and the aunts and the aging cousins who would read to me and tell her I was sweet—that at an age when no child isn't— but you wouldn't find me once in her description. You would find a rubber doll, stamped out and indistinguishable from a hundred others who would fit the doll clothes and the playhouse. My mother didn't know me."

"And that was her responsibility," Bea said. "She was in charge of knowing you, and carrying that knowledge around with her everywhere she went, besides the bags of groceries, and the other babies, and the worries, and the rest."

"How do you know what it was like for her?" Mattie broke in.

"I know," Bea said. "I know. I'm old now, but I was your age once, and younger still sometime before that. I'm old, but I was a mother. Jeannie pooh poohs the ironing and the laundry, and the putting up tomatoes and the grape preserves, and the white shoe polish—bottles of it—and the chicken pox and tonsils and the measles and the dogs getting sick in the middle of the kitchen Christmas Eve. Any time there's ever been a mention of the clothing and the shampoos, and the school notes, and the band concerts, and the girl scouts, Jeannie will get this glazed-over look in her eye, and I'm bright enough to pick up that she takes these carloads of particulars as what was there to be taken for granted, and that what we are supposed to talk about was what she didn't get, and how I let her down. That she and I weren't on the same wavelength, that I wasn't tuned in to her frequency. Well maybe, just maybe, consider it, she was not tuned in to mine. Are you a mother?"

"Yes," Mattie said.

"And are you setting the world on fire?"

Mattie let the air out through her nose. "I sure thought so for a while. At the start, for months, maybe into years, I sure thought so."

"And so did I," Bea said. "And so did your mother, rest her soul. And rest her body, too, and may somebody, somewhere, say to her this afternoon, she did just fine."

"You're saying it was me." Mattie made a point of not looking back at Bea. "You're saying I expected too much, had unrealistic ideas of what it was she should have given me. You're saying that making pies and ironing clothes and giving everybody a shampoo on Saturday nights was enough."

"I'm saying that it was a lot more than you think. I'm telling you I think there's room inside this car for a little bit of charity, and most of it in the front seat."

Mattie didn't feel enamored of any member of this trio, but she hated being clumped together with Jeannie most of all. Jeannie was a cold fish.

"See," Jeannie said. "You always loved Babette best." The cold fish giving voice to Mattie's sentiment again, accusing Mattie's absent mother on a second count.

"You've got it wrong there, Jeannie," Bea said. "I always loved you best, from the first moment I laid eyes on you until today, and probably until the day I die. And I have always *liked* Babette more than you. So there you have it, both of you."

Mattie thought it was as though Bea had just given her daughters each a family heirloom. One, an old ring set in platinum, with tiny diamonds, two or three dozen stones laid in a handsome pattern; and one, a single stone, heavy and elegant. And each girl would want the one she didn't have. Give the mother now a bag of stones, and let her keep handing jewels to them: necklaces with emeralds, precious stones, tiaras, bracelets, and they sit there with their hands out. Waiting. Not enough. Not satisfied. Finally, the bag empty. The floor littered with the heirlooms, things passed down from generation to generation, and there beside the jewels, the "Not enough's," the "But you never gave me's," the "But you didn't care's." All the things that hadn't been delivered, all the longing, lying mixed among the treasures there.

Maybe that was it. Mattie's thoughts spun out. You don't have what you need. It's obvious. Something's missing. You can feel it. Missing in your life. Missing in yourself. You were not given something that you wish you had, something you know you need. And you look around for somebody to blame. And guess who's there. Guess who's always been there.

No. It couldn't be that simple. There were gaps. Real gaping holes, needs not met, promises not kept, balls dropped, lives dropped, along the way. Forget about intent. No matter. It did happen, planned or not. And the victims are left alive to wonder, to be puzzled, if they ever stop to think it out. The rest of the time, they walk around not feeling entirely put together, always with this secret feeling they are faking it, making it up as they go along. While everybody else is solid, all filled in.

Like the Babettes. Babette didn't give off vibes that she was feeling particularly cheated, that she felt she had missed out. But that was Babette. What did she require for her soul? No, it was the Jeannies and the Matties who walked around crippled, disabled by the knowing something was missing.

I'm injured, Mattie thought. I'm wounded. So what if it happened a third of a century ago. I still feel the pain.

She was surprised, astonished even in broad daylight, that other people, people she knew well, people she had grown up knowing, had been done to by their mothers worse, far worse, than she, and they had gotten up, brushed the cinders from their hair, shaken themselves off, and the same day were getting on with things: getting on with life, with grocery shopping, bearing children, having complicated conversations and relationships with friends they met at every life stage along the way.

Mary Rhodes. Her mother had a stroke at the age of forty-seven. Mary was thirteen. "I don't mind for myself," Mary's mother slurred the words, "but I do hate to spoil your weekend." World-class martyr, she had recovered. Mattie thought that it was out of spite. And now, at seventy-eight, Mary's mother was in diapers, living in the new addition that was once Mary's backyard: the wallpapered bedroom with the oversize new bath with guard rails on the walls that represented the last of Mary's life savings, plus a second mortgage on her house. Mary's mother at seventy-eight, living in the bedroom, hobbling frail and birdboned out to the kitchen, asking Mary—mother leaning, listing by the stove—"Where is your mother? Why isn't she helping you?" There, and gone that far away.

Mary's mother had been unrelenting all the years that they were growing up. Imperious and cold. Demanding Mary be perfect the first time, every time. And Mary never winced, never withered under words that would have floored Mattie; Mary never even wondered at it much, not so far as Mattie could tell. Mattie, who even now would talk with Mary on the telephone some nights long after everybody else had been asleep for hours, everybody in the universe. They still spoke on the phone, unmonitored at this age, no longer lapsing into first-year French each time a mother walked into the kitchen. No need for French now: Mattie's mother had never been inside the kitchen in the house where Mattie lived now, and Mary's mother would no longer comprehend their English.

But not once, in any language, had Mary complained of her treatment at her mother's hand. She hadn't seemed to notice, hadn't known she was the injured party, entitled to some damages, or reparations.

Mary Rhodes told the mother stories everybody tells, then shrugged, raised one plucked eyebrow, took a long puff on a slim woman's cigarette, and gave a long exhale, and said, "So, Mattie, what's new at your end?" And when she wasn't on the telephone with Mattie, she was getting on with it: making tracks, going somewhere, never saying it out in so many words (that tells the whole thing for a lie), but just living it, a life she liked, a life she was getting a lot of pleasure from. Not a bit like Mattie, sitting quiet, nursing scars, old wounds, or the places she was almost certain wounds or scars would be if you could only see them. Being injured. Making a career of it. An occupation: My mother did me wrong. You get something out of that, or you don't do it forty years.

Just yesterday, a friend, Eileen, told Mattie she had just had a visit from a friend from Boston, and the friend's sister. "The sister's always been uptight, intense, every minute, worrying life, and my friend's so carefree and so happy," Eileen said.

"What makes the difference, if they're sisters?" Mattie asked Eileen. "What makes the difference? Is it chemistry or what?" She really did want to know.

Why is it one child shrugs off the family lunacy, hardly seems to register it at all, while all the Matties thrive on past injuries. Some of the wounded walk away, and others crawl to cover where they lick their wounds in quiet, and some stay stuck right there on the spot and say to anyone who'll listen, and to some who won't, "Look what was done to me. In this very spot. My mother never liked me."

My mother never liked me, Mattie thought. I never liked my mother, if it came to that. Those were the flip sides of the single coin she carried in her pocket everywhere, carried with no other coins to jingle it against, to make a noise or music with.

Her mother never loved her properly, as she required: the fatal flaw, the rotten core, the sponge-rubber foundation, the impasse, the burden so cumbersome, so debilitating, the burden so familiar, but too prized, somehow, to be put down here by the edge of the roadway, to be dropped for good. Mattie took it with her everywhere; because of it she came home early, turned down invitations, stayed away. With other people, she did not feel herself at ease, not often, never, without taking note. She had set up camp around the idea, at first a temporary thing, but as time went on, the structures she erected were more solid, more confining and familiar—known in every aspect—more reliable, to be relied upon. The handicap that will not desert you, that will never let you down.

And the real question, Mattie thought, the one that I will not consider, is why I won't let go, why I'm hanging on for dear life.

CHAPTER NINE

MATTIE REALIZED THE four of them had been riding silently for a long time: Babette with her chewing gum, Jeannie sealed up inside herself, Bea off somewhere. Nobody was standing in line to give you any answers.

"So," Mattie said. "What about your part, Bea?" Mattie summoned Bea back with a sudden urgency. "What about you? Are you happy with them? How is it the other way around? Did anyone cheat you? Did your girls turn out to be what you had in mind?"

Mattie had judged the crowd correctly. Neither sister spoke.

"I don't have what you'd call a major problem with either one of them," Bea said. "So maybe they're not the exact image of the way I would have designed them, left entirely to my own devices, but I take the good in together with the bad.

Jeannie's not got a joy in living that I mighta' wished she had, and she and I aren't likely to watch the same shows on TV, but she does an important job, and she does it real well. She takes on the responsibility to handle other people's living and their dying, and not everybody would sign up for that. I take Jeannie as she is."

"And Babette?" Mattie was no longer gunning for Babette. She honestly wanted to find out. Is every soul worth redemption? Mattie had thought Babette might be asleep, but she heard a sound, something like a word, enough to signal Babette was awake and paying attention.

"Babette is what she is, too," Bea said. "Same story, just a different character. Good and bad together. I know she's silly and light-hearted and she likes her clothes and money and her things, and I also know she let them take one of her kidneys to give to a boy who was eleven who would have died without it, and he wasn't even a relation. And I could swear that I have never heard her mention it, and it's been a few years now. And I could tell you for a fact that I would not have done it."

"I hate that," Mattie said. "I hate that. People have been pulling these stories on me all my life. Just when you have somebody fixed in your mind, and you know exactly how you feel about them and what they've done, you get some story about them that turns you all inside out and makes you feel sorry for them."

"I'm not asking you to feel sorry for me," Babette said.

"No," Mattie said. "I don't think you are. You've done a lot of things today, but no, not that. It's just I can't keep anything settled in my mind. I mean, who the good guys and the bad guys are. Was it my mother or was it me? She threw a glass across the room when she was angry once. She was aiming at my brother's head. She was vicious to my sister when her first son was born. She was cruel. And I'm left here with all these stories I don't even feel like telling you about her. I'm bored with the whole thing, with all the stories that don't add up to anything, are inconclusive, if you tell them to anyone who's not a shrink, to anybody you're not paying large amounts of money to say, 'Yes, she sounds like a deeply disturbed woman, who was not much of a mother to you.'"

Mattie was winding down. She felt tired, as though she had done hard work today, outside in a brisk wind.

"Jeannie," Mattie said. "Do you have anything to say about all this?"

"No," Jeannie said. "I don't think I do."

Mattie let it be.

Maybe Jeannie was tired, too.

The light was gone, or all the light that mattered, from the cold November sky. Mattie didn't like to drive at night. There were all the lights of the oncoming cars, and you had fewer indications of where you were, and fewer landmarks on your way.

Babette gave some child one of her kidneys. What an unlikely story to superimpose on what there was to see. Maybe Bea was making it up. No, Jeannie would have said something. Jeannie. What was her redeeming feature? (Seems they each had been assigned one.) Oh yes. She did worthwhile work. Knocking people out, to use her mother's phrase.

"Where's your mother?" Babette did not have a pleasant speaking voice.

"I don't know. I guess they will have taken her to the funeral home by now."

"No," Babette said. "I mean what town."

"Oh. Granby."

"Where is that? How far from here?"

"Probably four hours. Maybe five." Mattie hadn't thought until this moment that at some point she would need to get herself from here to there.

"When will you go?" Babette said.

"Well, I don't know." Mattie had not considered it. Not once. It was as though at some point she had just stopped going home, just frozen time in place, forgotten all about the journey. She had collapsed in a heap on the sidewalk of her life and decided to no longer offer any resistance. People did that. They did it all the time, said Here's my life, you take over, see if you can do anything with it. It's beyond me.

"You could spend the night at my house," Babette said. "Start off in the morning as early as you want to. You shouldn't drive tonight."

"I could go to a motel," Mattie said. Her mind's eye canvassed the sixty-dollar room. Two double beds. Maybe two queen-size. A glass guaranteed germ-free by a white, blue-lettered tissue wrapper. A paper sash across the toilet seat—or had they stopped doing that?

"Now, what do you want to go to a motel for? I'll give you some supper. You'll get to meet my kids, and you'll have your own room. A regular guest room with a teak wood luggage rack we got when we went on a cruise to one of the islands, and a canopy bed with a real canopy."

Not to be confused with a fake canopy, Mattie thought. She didn't answer. Mattie could remember wanting a canopy bed all the years that she was growing up. Nancy got a canopy bed the week Mattie left for college.

Mattie saw the Palmer-Lewisburg exit sign. Two miles.

"I'll tell you what." Mattie could tell she had taken the three silent, maybe sleeping, riders by surprise. "I'll tell you what. I think I need to be starting off for Granby as soon as I drop you off. So tell me where I should go once we get near town."

The plan came to Mattie only as she spoke the words. It was time she was heading home. Enough detours, enough false starts and getting turned around and so distracted. Enough denying. Time to go. She would gladly have dropped her passengers at the end of the exit ramp. She felt the four of them all had taken full advantage of one another. They of her, and she of them. And enough, in this case, was plenty. She didn't want to get to know Jeannie any better than she did.

"Oh, that's not right," Bea said. The lengthy pause before she spoke had stolen the conviction from her words. "You can't go off on your own now. Not in the dark. You heard Babette say you could stay with her, and then start off early, nice and fresh. You could go right to sleep when we get back and leave before any of us is up in the morning."

"No, really. Thanks all the same. I do need to go now. I have to see my father. He was hurt in the accident and he'll be awake by morning."

"Well," Bea said. "If you're sure. We could give you some coffee. It wouldn't take us too long to make."

"No, thanks. I can stop along the way, and I'm really wide awake now."

It seemed to Mattie like a marriage where both parties have wanted out for years, but feel, for form's sake, the need to protest and camouflage whatever relief they might be anticipating once the day of their release arrives.

"Well, if you're sure," Bea repeated.

Mattie felt a little sad. This was how the whole thing was

going to end. Just fizzle out. She knew she would never see any one of them again. She would never come back to Palmer. It would always be as though Palmer was where her mother died. And she would never spy Jeannie bustling down Fifth Avenue at Christmastime, her arms full of packages and presents. She would never catch a glimpse of Babette waiting, but not patiently, in line at the aquarium in Boston. She would not spy Bea in the supermarket, from behind, bent over wet green vegetables. She would never see them anywhere, but she would, from time to time, and less often as the years went by, imagine that she did.

Mattie wished that somehow things could have been better with her and Bea and Babette and Jeannie. The whole day had been such a mess. There was no reason why when you found yourself thrown together for some reason with people who might not be your first choice for anything, you couldn't make the best of it, come away with something. Days like this might matter. Who could tell? There might be repercussions. Fallout. Reverberations.

"At Joe's is fine," Bea said. "We can get a ride there easy. Drop us off at Joe's. No need to park the car. We can hop right out. We sure do thank you for your kindness, and we're real sorry about your mother's passing."

"Yes," Babette said.

Jeannie might have been asleep.

"Yes, really," Babette said.

"You're very welcome," Mattie said.

Company manners all around. "My mother said to tell you I had a very nice time," a woman said one night to Mattie as she was saying good-night at the door after a dinner party.

Nothing of substance would now be said by any one of

them; they would say their good-byes overlapping one another, and that, as the man said, would be that.

Once she could see the door, once her route of escape was not only established but all but guaranteed, Mattie wished more strongly to go back and do it over, or at least to sit down with the three of them and explain.

Such wishes often took the form of thinking she would do well to have a personal explainer, an interpreter: not for language, but for her moods and her behavior. Mattie wished she had someone to travel around with her to offer her excuses. She usually had purse and pockets full of them but never found occasion to present them on her own behalf.

Mattie thought that she would like a person who would go around with her explaining that Mattie was well aware of her behavior, her easy brusqueness, a sometimes impatience dressed up as rudeness—no other word for it. People had no idea that Mattie often saw herself almost exactly as they did. People think that if you realize what you're like, then you can change one day, just choose to be some other way, like, say, easygoing, remarkably pleasant, laid-back. Therapists perpetuate the notion of this facile possibility of change, they decorate their gray-and-pale-beige consulting rooms with the idea, write articles they get no compensation for, to publish the idea in journals, which will be read only by people already married and in bed with the idea.

Mattie would be happy if this person, this personal interpreter would now take a moment to explain to Bea and Babette and Jeannie that Mattie didn't really mean to judge them as harshly as it seemed. This bearer of explanations and apologies would say, "You must excuse her. Mattie means no harm—if she did, she would say so. Please know she can't help it. You see, there was a situation, or more likely several, when she was very small, that made her feel she was in some danger—in fact, she may have been—so she developed a sort of vigilance for detail way back then. A watchdog mentality. And if you give her half a chance, and if she likes you (you will know) why then, as time goes on you'll see she has less and less to say about what you should do and why and how and when—unless, of course, you are a relative." Mattie wouldn't want her interpreter trying to explain her to her family. They wouldn't listen anyway. They *knew* her. Any one of them would tell you that.

"Right here's fine," Bea's voice was casual, considering.

Mattie made a stop on short notice.

"Thanks a lot, really," Babette said. "If you're ever here again, come see us now." She was out the door.

"Take it easy driving. Pull over if you're sleepy." Jeannie's words sounded important, her message well thought out. Mattie felt as though she were leaving on a space shuttle. Solo. But then, the send-off would probably sound more offhand, the good-byes more cavalier.

CHAPTER TEN

MATTIE PULLED HER car into the middle of three vacant slots and turned off the ignition. She had been driving for a lifetime and it was only 6:15. Mattie blinked hard as he approached the building, moving closer to the source of the unnatural blue-cast light. Her eyes weren't making the transition very well.

Mattie stopped just before she reached the building. A burly man pushed through the door and barreled down the walk. Mattie was convinced he would have gone directly through her had she been standing in his way. It never failed. Once you got within forty yards of a McDonald's or a Howard Johnson's at a rest stop on an interstate, people became dehumanized, no longer civilized. Not personal. Not people. They behaved like so many blind automatons who would unbend with effort from their

low-slung cars, hobble across the parking lot through the gaso-
line-thick air, and straining, pull open the door, tucking shirttails
in, and, as if programmed, make a beeline for the restroom, always
sex appropriate. Then they moved to the restaurant counter for a
sandwich or a drink, or back out to the car.

People never spoke to strangers in these places, never
smiled, in fact, did not give evidence of seeing you at all. If you
meet a stranger in a tiny, overdecorated powder room of a
restaurant, she will always have something to say about the
potted plants or paper towel dispenser. Or in the restroom in a
church, or any public building with a children's fair, people
always speak, just as they do when you go to vote, or while you
wait in line to buy a raffle ticket for a handmade quilt. People
pass the time of day. But never at a rest area on an interstate.
Everyone's just passing through. They do what they came for,
stretch their legs, look without seeing at the gift shop souvenirs
imprinted for all time with the name of whatever state they're
in, and then yawn widely, not covering their mouths, and get
back to the car and drive off to a place where they will be
human, friendly, even conversational. They drive off to a destination where they will say hello to people they have never
seen before, people they may never see again.

Someone should do a sociological study about the ways that
situations and certain kinds of buildings influence the way
people treat one another, Mattie thought. Maybe someone
already has. Mattie stepped forward, pulling open the heavy
outer door. A fat woman charged out, oblivious, as though the
door had opened automatically.

Mattie went into the restroom. For the first time in memory
it was empty. The long rows of stalls with yellow metal doors
looked overly ambitious, perhaps a little lonely. Mattie came

out of the stall and washed her hands quickly. There were more than a few places Mattie didn't like to be alone.

She eyed the wall of telephones and vending machines. She had to call Paul, to tell him the news. He would be home by now. Telephones. A hardly satisfactory substitution for human contact, whatever the nostalgic New England Telephone ads lead you to believe. Mattie didn't want to make the call. It wouldn't make her feel any better. It would only emphasize exactly how alone she was, and she would feel the need to say in words the things she couldn't say. Maybe that was why she hadn't made the phone call until now. Maybe certain things would not be true until she put them into words and spoke the words out loud to Paul.

Her eyes moved over every row in each of the vending machine. All the usual suspects: M & Ms, Snickers, Baby Ruth, Mars bars, and the kind of LifeSavers they sell in these machines but nowhere else. Chips and corn curls, pretzels, Cheez-its, Chee-tos. No Zagnuts. Mattie didn't see a thing she wanted. Strangers milled around the area, aimless for the moment, as though waiting for an announcement saying it was time to get back in their cars and drive again.

Mattie called collect. Such a formal undertaking. Will you accept the charges? You weren't allowed to speak at all if someone on the other end said no.

"Andy, this is Mom. You sound so grown up. I'm so glad to hear your voice."

"Yeah, well, Mike just broke my new Transformer and he's gonna buy me a new one or I'm gonna kill him, and I can't find one of my Joes. Rock Viper. The one with the snake that comes off separate."

"Well, ask Dad to help you look. Is Daddy there, sweetie? I

need to talk with him. I'll see you at Grandma's tomorrow night, okay?"

Andy dropped the receiver.

"Sorry, Mom. I'll get him. He's outside."

Mattie felt so homesick. She felt as though she hadn't seen the boys for days. She had hardly thought of them or Paul all day. It was as though the idea of them hadn't carried as far as the state line, as though the state of Pennsylvania weren't large enough to hold her ideas of her two families: the one she had sprung from, and the one that sprang from her.

But no, it wasn't the dimensions of the state. It was the overweening, all-consuming sometimes, size of the first family, so that even the idea of them, the very memories of relationships and conversations old a dozen years ago crowded every other idea out, left no room in Mattie's mind for the everyday things: Paul, the boys, her friends, the people that she knew, her life. Sometimes they seemed like just bit players, afterthoughts; on stage practically the whole of every act, they had so few lines to say.

Take a day, Mattie thought, and say it has been twenty-four hours long. Take away eight hours for sleep and eight more for things that no one can account for afterward, and then subtract the minutes wasted worrying old wrongs; or better, add them up: the stray seconds, all the minutes. Pile them up in heaps of sixties. All the time spent, frittered, lost, on ancient history, old exchanges no one else has any recollection of. Let someone else go through your thoughts for the entire expanse of one afternoon, and let that stranger tally minutes spent on "Life Now Today," without transference, reference to the past, and all the minutes spent on "Life Not Today," life then. The fractions would amaze.

I hang out back there, Mattie thought. I'm like some teenager with time on his hands, who stands too often and too long outside a corner grocery store with people he doesn't much care for, exchanging ideas he has no interest in. I'm like a widow, old and withered, who lives alone with just her cat. She has a black-and-white TV that only works now when it's played with the VCR, and she owns only one videotape, a movie that she watches every day. She walks in on it at any point, wanders from the room in the middle of the major crisis scene. It doesn't matter. She has it memorized and often pays it no attention anyway, just keeps it running for the company, out of habit more than anything.

"Mattie. How are you? Are you okay?" Paul's voice sounded sweet and warm and service-worthy all at the same time, and very far away. "I called Nancy just a little while ago. I know about your mother. Mattie, I'm so sorry."

"Oh, you called. What did Nancy say?"

"She told me about your mother. I told her I was bringing the boys down tomorrow. Are you okay?"

"I don't know. I don't think I'm handling this thing at all in the regular way. In fact, I might not be handling it at all. I just drove three weird women back from Harrisburg, and before that someone pregnant almost had a baby in my car."

"What? Harrisburg? Where are you now?"

"I don't know. Probably about where I would have been at noon today if I'd taken 80 West instead of 80 East." Mattie thought, It's like my life: I'm where I would have been at twenty-seven if I hadn't missed my turn.

"Oh, Mattie. Poor Mattie. Are you staying over somewhere? Don't drive tonight. We'll leave early in the morning. We should be in Granby by midafternoon. Five at the latest. Do you need me to bring anything?"

"I must need a dress to wear. A black dress. Black shoes. Black hat with a veil. Black gloves. Black purse." Mattie saw the Italian Mafia widows in the Godfather movies: pure olive skin, lipstick bright red; all the rest, rich black.

"So what should I bring?" Paul said.

"Oh, Paul, you're so good to me. You've always been so good to me. Brings lots of toys, and books, for the boys in the car, and clean socks and extra shoes and church clothes, and try to find Andy's Rock Viper and my black dress with the red belt. It's the only black I've got. I don't own any gloves. I used to have six or eight pairs when I was little. We used to dye white cotton gloves to match our Easter outfits. I dyed mine orange one time, pale orange, the color of Creamsicles."

"Mattie, find a place to stay," Paul said. "Don't drive anymore tonight. It's too late."

"Are the boys okay?"

"Yes. They're fine. We had a good day. Andy's tired, and I think Mike's asleep."

"Well, try to find Andy's Rock Viper. He won't forget. I wonder if it's in my car. It might be here with me. Hang on, let me run out now and see if I have it with me in the car."

"No, Mattie," Paul said. "We'll find it. Don't worry. I'll look for it."

How will you find it, Mattie wondered, if it's here with me.

"I have to hang up now," Mattie said. "I think I must be tired. I don't know where everyone has gone. It was so crowded here when I first called you. I'm at a rest stop on Route Eighty. I'm pretty sure I didn't love her, Paul. I'm almost sure I didn't."

"Mattie, don't try to sort it out this late. Go find a motel. Get some sleep. You'll feel a lot better with some sleep. I love you, Mattie."

"I don't know why you do," she said. "I love you, too. I'll see you in Granby. Come to Nancy's house. I'll be there or at the hospital with Dad. Don't forget juice boxes for the car and pretzels. Take two bags. They're in the pantry, and I think we have some string cheese left. I can't remember."

"It's okay, Mattie. I'll take care of everything."

It seemed to Mattie such a nice idea.

CHAPTER ELEVEN

Mattie felt her shoulders and her back and legs, each with separate, independent pains, even before she was fully awake. She opened her eyes. The room was dark, and Mattie had a distinct impression there had been some particular instruction she had been given last night when she was checking in. It was gone. Gone with any recollection of how she had found this place and settled in. Mattie had just been dreaming that her mother was alive. She was taking swimming lessons in the ocean, out in the middle of the Atlantic.

Mattie rolled over and pulled the covers over her head. She would have groaned had there been anybody there to hear. Someone had absconded with the options while she slept. There was nothing left to do. She couldn't get back to sleep, and she certainly couldn't get out of bed. She couldn't just lie here, or not indefinitely, unless she put another sixty dollars in the meter every morning, and called up Nancy to say she would never be coming home. All the choices were precluded, each by a separate impossibility, its own individual way of being unthinkable.

Maybe there were choices she hadn't considered, some alternative, something other than the usual that certain people found to do the morning of a mother's funeral, in the restless, senseless hours everybody waits through until the moment they have all agreed upon, to say the words and sing the hymns that the deceased decided on when she was sick with nothing anyone remembers back in 1964. The moment when they put her in the ground. Now there's the thought you want to go eyeball to eyeball with in order to assure yourself you'll make it through the afternoon.

Alternatives, Mattie thought. That's what we're lacking here. Short of hiding underneath the bed, or passing the day stretched out in the backseat of her car, Mattie drew a blank. She could just start off, get some breakfast, and stop for the first hitchhiker who didn't look like an ax murderer, and take him wherever he wanted to go. She could drop him off in California, then stop somewhere for coffee and regroup. But her luck, any hitchhiker who came her way would be a blood relative of Bea and Babette and Sherry Hicks, who was no doubt by this time no longer pregnant. Her child would be hours old, already hard at work on fashioning a personality, a temperament, a way of being that would have to last him eighty years.

Mattie dragged herself out of bed. Her body, lately, was a creaky sixty-five, at least until she had been upright ten or fifteen minutes. Coffee, under the right conditions, and she could get the numbers down to fifty-five or fifty, but the last reduction, to a limber forty-four, was less predictable.

Mattie pulled off the gray sweatshirt she had slept in, took a two-minute shower in the tepid water, and dressed in her clothing from the day before. She would have loved a bath, but even the idea felt too much like settling in. If she stuck around even long enough to find fresh clothes, and do her face, she might never leave. She would grow old and die in this motel.

In the office Mattie got a Styrofoam cup of something that smelled a lot like coffee from across the room, but passed up the doughnuts with the plastic sugar glaze.

Sitting in the driver's seat, it seemed that she had never stopped at all but had driven through the night and through her sleepiness until she had come out the other end, no longer sleepy, but something infinitely worse. Mattie nursed her coffee, and when it was all gone, she went back to the unattended office and grabbed her room key, and went back to her room and brushed her teeth, violating a cardinal rule of the open road: Once you check out, you don't go back to your room, for anything.

Once more on the highway, Mattie felt just shy of resourceful. Probably the toothpaste. Sometimes just a scent of something, or a taste, can make you feel as though you just might make it through the next half hour.

But Mattie's head felt like a sieve. Not the tin one that first came to mind, but like a bright green, inexpensive plastic one that would break the first time someone stepped on it. Thoughts, images of trees and grass and sky, flashes of fabric in pastels that pass for shrouds, Paul and the boys still fast asleep, the lump-lump of the tar stripes on the road, all passed through the plastic sieve like Play-Doh pushed by little fingers through the hundred tiny holes. And then, for miles, there was no thought at all.

At one point, Mattie wondered if she had actually been asleep. You read about that happening. Mattie had heard once that a navigator on a 747 woke up with a jolt, midway over the Atlantic, and found the pilot and the copilot in the cockpit fast asleep.

Miles. More miles. Mattie looked for the alphabet on license plates but stopped before she got to C. She had always hated that game, even as a child. There were no road signs. Only trees. One empty road. One empty woman.

Mattie was in a bind. She couldn't take much more of this drive; at the same time she wanted never to arrive, to get back, not to what was there but back there to what had never been. To the mother, then as now, who was nowhere there.

Her absence had been palpable; what was missing as concrete as the red-and-white, plastic-coated carton of milk in the refrigerator that is empty when you go to pour—more absent for the expectation. The lacking was as real as the quiet of a house at three o'clock in the afternoon when you can tell that no one's home, even though you were expected, and you stand, odd and alone, listening to the hollow ringing of a telephone through empty rooms. What was missing was fleshed out, as known as the blind date who never shows, as cold as the sheets on the other side of the bed the first night your husband stays away all night, you don't know where, as real as the sealed envelope you open up to find the letter missing, as frightening as the funerals you buy black dresses for in your imagination.

One whole childhood, made of pieced-together gaps, so that there will be nothing useful you can draw upon when you are expected by yourself and everybody else to get along, so that you rely upon the deficits, you use the lacking for foundation stones, and what was missing for the mortar.

Absence. Palpable. Concrete. As concrete as the mother who stood ironing, who stooped scrubbing, who bent lifting, who said no more than three or four phrases you remember from an episode that lasted eighteen years, the mother who was there every day, all day, all of your life, the mother who was never there. A person will remember that and feel it as a thing, will call the memory back, or meet it uninvited on the stairs.

Or maybe Mattie had gotten it all wrong, maybe she could hack back through the bramble and the bracken, grown so thick with years. Track fast enough to surprise some early version of herself and this mother there together, poised and teetering on the brink of that false step that ever after did define their ways.

It had been only last year that Mattie's mother had unwittingly offered up a clue. She had been stretched out on the bed in the room where Mattie had slept as a child. Mattie's sons Andy and Mike had been hanging around, cracking bubble gum, examining the knickknacks on the bureau, half-listening to Mattie and her mother's aimless chat.

"We drove today to where the elementary school was when I was in the first grade," Mattie had said to her mother. "It was one-point-three miles, one way. We clocked it. And I would have had to cross Chestnut Street, which was like a superhighway, to get there. I walked all by myself. Do you remember? I was only six years old. The boys couldn't believe it."

Actually, the boys had believed it with no trouble, they just didn't see what all the fuss was about.

"I walked two-point-six miles there and back every day," Mattie had said.

"Did you really?" Mattie's mother had said, a stranger, being polite. "Do you know, when you were in the first grade, the teacher asked me one day would I bake cookies for the class. I guess they asked all the mothers. They took turns and it was mine. Well, we had terrible ants then. They were everywhere and I was scared the ants would get into the cookies in the night, so I wrapped them up in wax paper and put them in a skillet with a lid and then I took ant powder and put it on the counter the whole way around the cookies. I was so afraid they wouldn't be all right."

Mattie had never heard the story before. She knew of only one incident from that time. Two aunts had come from out of town to visit, and Mattie's mother put four empty cooking pots with covers in the refrigerator to make it look like there was some food on the empty shelves. It wasn't the memory of her family's need that hardened to a lump in Mattie's throat, it was her mother's childlike effort to fool the snoopy aunts with empty pots and pans.

Then to be told this ant-powder story forty years after it happened. It broke Mattie's heart. It made her wonder, what if she had stood watching from the doorway that night to see her mother brush ant-powder into a tiny mountain range surrounding those already so-protected cookies? What if she had not only seen but understood the act to be the anxious taking-care, the frightened effort that it was, had seen this twenty-four-year-old, so timid and so worried about how her cookies and her self would measure up against the expectations of the first-grade teacher?

What if early on, Mattie had been given to see the soft underbelly skin, the timid young woman, barely holding poverty at bay, and trying to create a self that she could take to church and to the grocery store and not be made to feel that she was shabby goods by the other mothers or the principal or the mean quartet of neighbor ladies who snubbed her at the PTA. Those small-town, 1950s ladies of position, whose only claim to social standing lay in the fact that their husbands worked in banks with other people's dollar bills, or wrote wills and defended criminals, or took care of people's rheumatism and their hemorrhoids and whooping cough. These ladies who with all their might tried so hard to be pretentious.

What if Mattie had seen and understood all that?

But it doesn't work that way. Mattie was a child with puzzlements and problems of her own, a forty-four-pound person with 2.6 miles to walk to school and back each day, with busy streets to cross, bullies in the neighborhood to best, her own fears and worries to contend with all alone: an angry mother to come home to after school.

Mattie and her mother were like two prisoners in Siberia, far too busy and too cold to look around and see the other person was all tuckered out and shivering too.

Mattie was a child, how could she know an angry mother is a thing not born that way, but made, of equal parts of fear and disappointment, loneliness and some bewilderment mixed in with just enough tough stuff inside to voice a serious protest, shake a mean fist at the sky, and raise a little rumpus.

Shouldn't understanding count for something even here today? No, Mattie thought. Douse understanding with three cans of kerosene and burn the whole thing up. It doesn't matter if you understand a thing to death. You still need the people in your family to be kind to you, and almost every day. Especially people like your mother.

Mattie had sat at the bottom of that bed last year and listened to her mother's story. No doubt it was the very bed that she herself had slept in, breathing shallow, dream-dense sleep, the night her mother stayed up late protecting cookies in the kitchen. The place, the room, was the same room as that night. The only difference was that thirty-eight fast years had passed. So what if, Mattie thought, you could make a bracelet of the years, a circle of the thing. Not this long straight line, but a perfect circle round. Why then the distance between any two parts would be reasonable to travel, not too far away, but held together in the circle of the bracelet. And nothing would be lost. It could be a charm bracelet, Mattie thought, the kind with a tiny ballerina and a bicycle and a tin fan that closed and opened and miniature scissors that could really cut. And if there was a charm for everything that happened, then through the day, at odd moments, you could finger one charm or another, idly diddle it between two fingers, ping it with your fingernail, but only as a sideline, leaving all the rest of you free for other occupation: for long, complicated, interesting conversations, for heart-to-hearts with your best friend, and ferris wheels, and prayer, and étouffée, and calla lilies, and long belly laughs at really funny jokes.

Make a bracelet like that if you can. Have a hundred jewelers work all night. And make a million. Everyone will want one.

"Bbbbbbbbbbbbbbbb." Mattie made the silly lip sound every infant knows. That standard first accomplishment, what mothers and their babies do in strict rotation when they are alone in the kitchen, and everybody else is off somewhere doing something with adults, something there's a name for, something that can be described in words.

Mattie hit the brakes and slowed the car sufficiently to make the turnoff for the rest area. She attempted to hold her head in

such a way to make the honking driver in the car behind her
think she knew precisely what she was about. Mattie pulled up
beside a picnic table. She stretched her every part unbending
from the car, and walked over and sat down at the empty picnic
bench. There were families everywhere.

Where did these people get their clothing? Who dressed
them? Maybe Babette was on to something. Approximately
one person in two hundred wears anything becoming, if you
don't count anyone who is rail thin and under twenty-two.
Mattie started counting polyester windbreakers. She got to
fourteen and put her head down on the picnic-table bench,
curling up her legs for balance. The sun felt wonderful. The sun
today shone without any rays of danger, the cool morning air
a filter allowing only healthy rays to penetrate the atmosphere.
The sun was only good for you today. Mattie was asleep.

She dreamed she walked across a beach entirely covered
with green sea urchins, and not one of them would crack, no
matter how you stepped. They were like cobblestones beneath
her tennis shoes, and you could see that they continued everywhere, were even covering the bottom of the sea. The water in
the ocean didn't move; there was no lapping on the shore.
Then Mattie was fighting with her sister, Nancy, a fistfight,
with strong, hard, sudden blows that felt the same to you if you
were striking or receiving. A phone rang and the fighting
stopped, and Mattie went to answer it. It was her mother. She
said Nancy had just died. She had been eaten by an alligator at
a camping site in a state park in Florida.

Mattie started to roll over, caught herself, and brought her
feet down first, just barely missing falling off the bench. She sat
up, feeling drunk, then got up and wobbled off in the direction of the building, her legs behaving in a more usual fashion

as she went along. Inside, she washed her face, and then her hands, holding them for a long time under the hot water. She could still smell the soap from the dispenser as she passed through the busy corridor.

As she approached the car, Mattie realized that the lenses of her glasses were coated over with an almost even film of grease. She took them off, managing to get the key into the lock without actually seeing. The door wasn't even locked. Mattie sat a long time, breathing, fogging up her glasses, wiping them.

CHAPTER TWELVE

WHAT TIME WAS it? What day? The hours up to their old tricks again, their old deceivings. There are hours, Mattie thought, that march like Sherman to the sea, and hours you must carry on your back in scratchy burlap sacks that bulge with rocks shaped like potatoes. There are hours that are tiny balls of mercury from old, broken thermometers that you must sweep together in a pile, hours, slippery balls of mercury, that tease and trick your broom. Hours that evaporate like turnip water you've forgotten on the stove. There are hours that know you as the border collie doing what border collies do, with just the same amount of shepherding and barking, but with not so much success.

Mattie reached down for her food bag on the floor. She fumbled through the bag, then frowned. She was sure there was a box of Triscuits somewhere. Mattie eyed the traffic and the road ahead, then turned her head around to look in the backseat. Lying sound asleep, a little girl with an amazing head of light blond curls reached up and brushed an open hand across her cheek. It seemed she moved to brush off Mattie's gaze.

Mattie's heart was pounding like she had just driven into a brick wall. She looked front, then backward two more times and slowed the car to pull off onto the shoulder of the road. Mattie shut off the ignition, turning around to look at the little girl. She couldn't have been more than five or six. Mattie had two sons and had always said that God knew what He was about not giving her a daughter, since the female-parent female-child arrangement hadn't been what anyone would call an unqualified success the first time around. But Mattie would have signed up for this little girl, no questions asked.

But where on earth had she come from? How had she ended up, asleep, in Mattie's backseat?

Mattie turned more fully in her seat to watch the sleeping child, to see, then wonder if she saw, the shallow breathing in and out, the lips closed lightly, eyelids relaxed, nothing tight or strained in any way. Lift a limb, select any one at random, and it flops like a rag doll, but more weighty, more dead-weight. Watching sleeping children, an occupation she was practiced at.

When her sons were infants, Mattie went into their rooms at night, before she went to bed, and held a single finger, mustache angle, underneath the nose, to feel the warm breath there. Later, when the boys were out of babyhood, she watched them sleep, their bodies longer than in daylight, older-looking, lying, sprawling, out from underneath the covers always. And she would think to talk to them, to wake them up.

At first, it is enough the baby is alive, and sleep hard-won and unreliable you do not look to disarrange. But later, Mattie would watch the sleeping Andy and want him fully conscious and awake, sleep-warm and cuddly, hugging back. Talking husky, slow sleep-talk, words from dreams he won't remember with the light. Wide awake, together in the middle of the night the way you never ever are together in the day.

Mattie wanted to wake him up and tell him, "I'm sorry there has been so little us together, and so much else today: mechanics and gyrations." She wanted to shake his bony shoulder, to wake him up to say, "I'm sorry, don't grow up this way. Let's stop the clock and do it right. Let's sit and chat together now. Let's sit here by the campfire that we'll build so late tonight, and roast marshmallows crispy, burnt black to remembering, and take away from being here whatever you will need, what years from now will keep you dry and warm in heavy storms, and safe when lightning and the thunder come as one together."

Mattie wished that she could say, "I love you in a way that you will never know about. It's buried under piles of laundry and our history, and the rules and habits we have set up to navigate somehow from breakfast through to suppertime." There's so much regret to parenting, even when you're in the middle of the thing.

Mattie had intended this life differently, had intended that the childhoods of her children be some clean, well-lighted place, with treehouses full of blood-brothers, dinner with food children like to eat every night at six o'clock, and no one ever cross. Mattie had intended herself never to be cross, or certainly not cross sometime every day. She had intended leisure, forethought, raising children who would grow up to be kind, gracious people with a strain of courtesy running to the core.

She had not counted on this off-the-cuff life, but rather something steady, well thought out, a life that looked to all appearances as though someone had planned to live it just that way. She had not calculated on this blindfolded, or at the very least, distracted, one-arm-tied-behind-your-back kind of life, a life lived while you were obviously thinking about something else.

A family can be such a makeshift thing, until the kids are grown and moved away, and then you turn around, and memories are cast in stone, ensconced in places you never would have thought to put them down, not even for a moment, just to free your hands.

Mattie lay in bed some nights, after she had finished reading someone else's life all bundled up as fiction, lay in bed, and with something like surprise, would say, "Oh no," with all the force of conversation. "Oh no." This day wasn't what I had in mind at all. This phone call, errand, running-in-place day, during which I can remember doing not one thing I would say yes to in its contemplation, nothing with the boys, nothing with Paul, hardly anything alone even, with just myself. And then she rolled over in bed, and plumped her pillow, snuggled down, or tossed and turned a bit, and it was ten years later, and she would sit up in bed again, and say, "Oh no," with all the force of conversation.

Mattie had intended proper linens, sheets and towels, a houseful of things to go with the experiences, a house of things to match the people, things planned, things for a reason, not these random spoils of early marriages, one hers, one Paul's, both contracted at an age when people registered silver patterns, serving pieces, vases, bowls, and platters, because certain magazines said it was the thing to do. Mattie could see her silverware drawer, actually the drawer where knives and spoons and forks kept company with bottle openers, twist ties, magnets, spatulas, and candle pieces. There were people who had all these things sorted out, in separate places, slots where they could find each piece the first time they looked. These pieces, and the bowls and dishes, certainly the casseroles and big Dutch ovens, all had lasted longer than the early marriages. Most would outlive Paul and Mattie.

Mattie had seen a poster years ago that said, LIFE IS WHAT HAPPENS TO YOU WHILE YOU ARE MAKING OTHER PLANS. She hadn't bought the poster. Even then it was not new information. Still, late at night, not every night, but some nights, it would come again as a surprise. Oh no, this isn't what I had in mind at all. And all the people she might tell were sound asleep by then, beside her snoring in some way that was entirely familiar, or down the hall, or off somewhere, and maybe not asleep at all.

A tandem tractor trailer truck went by, and the whole car seemed to lift and fall. The little girl opened her eyes.

"Are you the babysitter?"

"Well, no, I'm not."

"Who are you?" The little girl sat up.

"My name is Mattie."

"What are you doing in my car? Where did the McDonald's go?"

"The McDonald's?"

"Yeah. My mom is still in there. I got too sleepy in the line, and she said to go out to the car and wait, and now I'm waiting. Where's my mom?"

Her words were not so much fearful as accusatory, not

worried for her own but for her mother's safety.

"Look. Everything will be fine. It must be that when you came out in the parking lot you got into the wrong car and fell asleep, and I came out and didn't see you and drove off. I will drive you back there now and I'm sure your mom will be right there waiting."

"I'm not allowed to ride with strangers. Not even if they say my mom sent them to pick me up to go buy ice cream, and especially not if they say will I get in their car with them to go and help them find their kitty. Not even to help them find their dog."

"I know, and that's exactly right. I'm a mom, too, and that is what I tell my kids, but I'm afraid we're a little stuck here." Mattie looked around and so did the little girl. She seemed to consider, then crawled into the front seat.

"Well, just don't try to offer me any candy."

"You got a deal."

The little girl buckled her seat belt like it wasn't the first time. Mattie saw a cutoff across the grassy median ahead and pulled in, waited for a break in traffic, then sped off in the direction she had come. And so, from now on she would just drive back and forth, and forth and back, crossing Pennsylvania forever, off on one fool's errand or another, taking daughters to their mothers, mothers to their little girls, and every single time it will seem a reasonable thing to do.

"Do you have any Barbies?" the girl asked.

"No," Mattie said. "No Barbies. How about you? Do you have any Barbies?"

"Nope. Me neither. My mom and I think they're sexist."

Mattie loved talking to anybody under the age of eight.

"What's that mean?" Mattie said.

"Boobs too big. Too pointy. You know."

"I know," Mattie said.

"Too bad you can't offer me anything I like in case you have it in the car. But I think we should stick to that rule. My mom and I like to stick to the rules a lot."

"Me too," Mattie said. She was pretty sure it was the truth.

"I always figured if I was ever kidnapped—not like this, but in the normal way—I would just say I wasn't hungry if I was offered any poison by the robbers. But then, if we stopped at a Friendly's or someplace, I would not say no if they tried to buy me an ice cream, because it's probably just about as safe as if you get an ice cream there when you're with someone you're related to. Unless, I thought, if they had a special box with ice cream that they sold to kidnappers who want to poison kids, but then how would they know which flavor you were going to ask for?"

"Right," Mattie said.

"So if you want to buy me an ice cream you can do it."

A police cruiser zoomed by doing seventy or eighty miles an hour. The car was out of sight in the time it took for Mattie to realize that the sensible thing to do was to turn this child over to a state trooper. They could contact the child's mother and could have the child back in half the driving time.

"Keep your eye out for a police car," Mattie said. "The policeman can drive you back."

"I'm only going back with you," the girl said. "You're the only one around here I'm riding with. Besides, my mom and I don't think much of policemen. We had a bad experience."

"What happened?"

"Oh, we knew a policeman once, Bob, but it didn't work out, and now we just look the other way whenever we see one."

"Well, a policeman could at least call your mom and tell her you're okay."

"Yeah well, fine. But I'm only riding back there with you."

Mattie spied a cruiser in the rearview mirror. She put her four-way flasher on and slowed to fifty-five. The cruiser overtook the two cars behind Mattie and then sped past.

"Damn," Mattie said.

She pulled into the passing lane and left her flasher on. She put her foot down. Sixty. Sixty-seven. Seventy. Seventy-three. Mattie liked the feeling of the speed. Seventy-seven. Eighty-one. The car felt a little wobbly. Not as solid as it did at seventy.

Eighty-one miles an hour. But no one was paying any attention. Mattie turned her lights on, hit her brights. No response. Maybe lights don't show up in the daytime. She eased off the gas. Seventy-six. Seventy. She had lost the cruiser.

"I can't believe this," Mattie said. "I got three speeding tickets yesterday. I couldn't go over fifty-four without getting picked up."

"We knew a man who had about a hundred parking tickets once, but now he lives in California."

"We'll just keep driving. We'll find another cruiser. I just don't want any more tickets."

"We don't need a policeman anyway. We'll get back to Mom just fine. You're a very good driver."

"Thanks." Mattie hated compliments, and she loved them. "You're a very good passenger."

"I know." The girl opened up the little canvas bag she held. Mattie tried to see inside but couldn't. She took out a drawing tablet and a purple marker, but only held them in her lap.

Mattie saw the sign, official in blue and gold: PENNSYLVANIA
STATE POLICE BARRACKS, NO. 917   OFFICIAL USE ONLY   NO
ACCESS. Not exactly the soul and spirit of hospitality.

Mattie took the turnoff. She would have driven on by, but
she had to let the mother know her daughter was okay, that
she could go back to breathing in and out without making
conscious effort, go back to fretting about the traffic or the
delay, switch back to being sane.

Mattie had always wondered what it would be like to drive
up to one of these places, out of uniform, arriving as a woman,
to smile and ask for directions to someplace in another state,
or for the correct time. They fortified these places, made it
clear with far too many signs, no visitors were welcome. We
don't give tours, lady. Keep driving.

Mattie parked and she and the little girl got out as if on cue.

"What's your name?" Mattie said. She felt as though she, or
maybe both of them, were guilty of a recent crime.

"Angelica."

"Nice. What else?"

"Melissa Perkins."

"Okay." Mattie smoothed her hair back with one flat hand
and ran her tongue across her upper teeth. "Okay."

Mattie could remember lying in bed beside her grandmother. She might have been the age of Angelica. It was the
middle of the afternoon, so someone must have needed or
been told to take a nap. Mattie lay there paralyzed, eyes open,
frozen in a stare. Her grandmother sound asleep beside her. A
deep sleep. Fortunately she lay between Mattie and the door.
Mattie had just come back from a party at a friend's house
where she had accidentally smashed a toy. (The broken toy was

gone. Crossing the parking lot with Angelica at her side, Mattie couldn't call back what it might have been.) But lying there, not listening to the Sunday sleeping breathing, Mattie knew the toy could never be repaired, and it was just a matter of time before they came to get her. She could hear their thick-soled, black, spit-shined boots sounding angry on the stairs. She could feel the door push open, the policeman—maybe with a deputy—barges in. (The grandmother snores on.) "You'll have to come with us now." Mattie in her nightgown led away. Life in prison. Maybe worse.

Mattie took Angelica by the hand. "Here, hold on," she said.

CHAPTER THIRTEEN

THE WOMAN SEATED at the desk was a surprise. Mattie was expecting a cloister of men.

"We're not open to the public." The woman's voice sounded like a computer. In fact, Mattie thought, if you had to pick someone who looked like a computer, you wouldn't cross this woman off your list, or not right away. "The sign out there tells you very clearly you're not supposed to stop here."

"Yes. I know," Mattie said. "But I didn't know how else to find a policeman. I chased a cruiser down Route Eighty going eighty-five, but I couldn't get anyone to notice me."

"The speed limit in Pennsylvania is fifty-five miles per hour."

"She knows that," Angelica said. "She's got three tickets."

"I have stopped here to report that I found this child, Angelica Perkins, in my backseat, and I assumed you could contact her mother right away to let her know that Angelica's with me."

The woman reached up and pushed a button on the wall. The sound it made was nasal and electric, and produced two men in uniform in short order. Call out the troopers. They were both enormous, bigger than life. Mattie's first husband had known a man in Buffalo who drove up to Toronto twice a week to have his body stretched, because he was a quarter of an inch too short to join the state police. You needed to be very tall.

"Tell these officers what you just told me," the woman said in her computer twang.

Mattie sighed. She should have stuck to chasing police cars.

"I stopped at a rest area, and when I came out to get into my car, my glasses were greasy and I was cleaning them as I got in and didn't see this little girl, Angelica, asleep in my backseat. She had gotten into my car by mistake. I figured you could track down the mother and tell her Angelica's okay. She was in the McDonald's at the last rest area, just east of here."

"Have we got an o-nine-four-ten-thirteen?" the older of the two men asked the human computer. He probably had seniority.

The woman tore the top sheet off a pad of printed forms. It was the only paper product on her desk.

"Please come with me." The man stepped back to allow Mattie to go first. She wasn't certain where to go or when to stop. This man probably still held the car door for his wife.

Fifteen unnecessary minutes later, the officer finally began his attempts to locate Angelica's mother. Mattie slipped out of the office and started down the corridor toward the pay phone.

"Miss." The second in command came running after her. "Miss."

"I'm just going to use the telephone."

Mattie felt as though she were in the military.

Angelica ran after her.

"Promise you won't leave me here," Angelica said.

"I won't leave you here."

"You'll stay until my mom comes. You remember we had a bad experience."

"I remember," Mattie said. "Now, go back in there and tell him you want to say hi to your mom."

Mattie dialed Nancy's number.

"Hello."

"Hello, is Nancy there? This is Mattie."

"Well, Mattie, I hate to be the one to tell you, but you got yourself the wrong number. Nancy who? I could know her."

"I'm sorry. Thanks."

Mattie dialed again.

"Nancy, it's Mattie."

"Mattie. Where are you? I was asleep. What time is it? Are you at Mum and Dad's?"

"No, I'm on the road. I'll be there in about three hours."

"Oh. You're still on the road. Where'd you sleep? They're going to operate on Dad at ten. He'll be okay. It's just something with his arm. I can't believe I was asleep. The doctor said it wasn't a major operation but that they needed to put him out, so he won't be back to his room for a few hours after that. So don't you rush now. Where are you calling from?"

"I'm at a state police barracks on Route Eighty. I'm not sure just where."

"I thought those places weren't open to the public. Are you okay all by yourself? It's awful for you to be alone now."

"Well, I've been meeting some people along the way."

"Oh, well, that's good. Now listen, Mattie, I know you won't like this, but we had to make all the funeral arrangements yesterday. I couldn't wait until you got here, and mostly I just told them the things I knew that mother wanted, but I did have to pick the dress. It's blue. Not navy, but real dark with some white around..."

"Nancy, you know, I don't think it's really hit me that she's dead yet. I never thought about her dying. I mean, she talked about it for the last twenty years, but I never really thought about it."

"Well, Mattie, some things we just don't comprehend. The Lord knows best about some things."

It seemed to Mattie that it wasn't out of the question that the Lord knew best about everything. So why did Nancy's words make Mattie cringe.

"Well, look. I'll be there before too long."

"I couldn't help it about having to pick out the dress by myself," Nancy said. "I couldn't wait. I told the undertaker that you would want a say."

"I have to go now, Nancy. Someone needs to use this phone."

Mattie walked quickly down the hall. She had a sudden flash fear that Angelica might have disappeared.

The little girl was up on her knees on a swivel chair, bent over a table, where she was drawing pictures of princesses in crowns, some in ballgowns, some in playclothes or swimsuits, but always with a crown. One princess held a crown in one hand and a tennis racquet in the other.

"Did you talk with your mom?" Mattie said.

"Yep. She's not too happy with you, but I told her we're doing fine here."

"Mrs. Welsh, we'll need to have you sign this statement. Mrs. Perkins is coming here to get the girl. She'll be here in half an hour."

"Any chance Angelica and I could duck into the nearest town for a quick ice cream while we wait?"

Angelica jumped down from the chair, folding up the princesses.

"I'm afraid that would not be possible," the policeman said.

"Because?" Mattie was fumbling in her purse to get her keys. "Because?" she repeated.

"Well, you see, Mrs. Welsh, she is under our jurisdiction now. We could not permit her leaving the premises with any unauthorized personnel."

Angelica pulled on Mattie's hand. "It's all right. We're not even positive we wanted to get ice cream. Remember how we said that in the car."

No lesser force could have kept Mattie from the fray.

"Come on." Angelica was all business. "We'll wait out in the hall."

Mattie hated authority figures. Anyone with temporary permission to tell you what you could or couldn't do. People in offices whose job it was to say, "I'm sorry but," the ones who took real pleasure in their work, telling people in predicaments: No, you can't, the rule is, the waiting period is, there are no exceptions—when, if life offers patent proof of anything, it is that there always are exceptions.

Mattie turned back and stuck her head around the corner of the office. "You think I'd kidnap her."

"Let's just say, we would not offer you the opportunity, Mrs. Welsh," the trooper said.

"You know," Mattie looked the state policeman in the eye. "I never liked Pennsylvania. Even as a child, I was never really happy here."

Mattie felt Angelica tugging on her hand again and allowed the little girl to lead her out into the hallway. She hated it when strangers called her Mrs. Welsh. It sounded like Paul's mother's name. And she especially hated it when strangers called her Mattie. Too familiar. Names were for later on. You worked up to them.

Mattie and Angelica sat down on a bench. The man in uniform peeked out around the corner. Mattie felt like she was going to cry. This might be—no, it was for certain—the last time she could ever take Angelica out for ice cream. In an hour she'd be gone. For good. Mattie didn't even know where.

"Where do you live?" Mattie said.

"Pittsburgh. Well, Fox Chapel. It's a part of it, but not the main part."

"Do you have a dad?"

"Not like regular. I have one, but he's not there. I see him two Saturdays in a month and he has a girlfriend, Mary, who gives you hamburgers on a bun made out of rocks. You can't even bite them."

"Do you have brothers or sisters?"

"Just a dog, and my mom says she would rather die than get a cat, so I don't think we'll probably be getting one."

"What's your mom like?"

Mattie sometimes quizzed the boys' friends over macaroni and cheese, sitting sipping coffee while they ate, offering seconds or dessert when they seemed forthcoming, chatting on, oblivious to editing or to effect, just saying out loud what was true. The crusade: to find out the secret, always up against the feeling other people's families did it in some other way, some way Mattie never would have thought of.

"My mom's pretty," Angelica said. "Blond hair. Honey Ash Blond is the name of it, and she's tall and she smokes cigarettes, but not all the time."

Angelica unfolded the paper with the princesses. She drew a large building enclosing them all.

Next question. What? Do you love her? Is she a good mother? Is she doing such a number on you that you won't realize it till you're in analysis at thirty-five? Or have you got one of the good ones? Does she bolster your self-confidence and show you how to be by how she is herself?

Angelica drew a picket fence around the princesses' house. It reached the roof line all around. Then she spent some minutes on elaboration: crenellation, chimney bricks, and flowers on the lawn, each one with individual petals.

"You want to leave?" Angelica said.

"No," Mattie said.

"You're getting restless."

"No."

"You seem to me like you want to hit the road, like maybe there is a place you need to get to before lunchtime."

"No," Mattie said. "I'm always like this."

"Oh." Angelica refolded the princesses and turned her back to Mattie, bent over, intent over her work.

She turned and handed Mattie the fat paper square. It said, "To Maddie W., From your friend, Angelica."

Mattie pushed her glasses up. Twice. "Is this for me?"

"You can show it to your kids," Angelica said. "Put it on your refrigerator if you have any magnets. But don't use tape. You'll ruin the grass."

"Magnets," Mattie said. "No tape. Come on. Let's walk around this place. See what there is to see. We might hit upon a candy machine. Maybe even find a Zagnut."

Mattie went through life in search of Zagnuts. She wasn't sure why she bothered. She hardly ever found one, and when she did, it was almost always stale. She wondered if somebody at the factory had a grudge, held onto them until they'd aged sufficiently.

Angelica and Mattie started down the hall.

"What's a Zagnut?" Angelica said.

"Oh, a Zagnut's wonderful. It's not like any other candy. Peanut butter and toasted coconut and no chocolate."

"I like chocolate," Angelica said.

"A lot of people do."

"I guess," Angelica said, "that this might be one of the safest places in America to buy a candy bar. I mean with all the policemen swooping around all over the place."

Mattie had only seen two so far. The halls and all the offices they passed were deserted. Mattie tried the door marked with the red-and-white lighted exit sign at the end of the corridor. It was locked. She tried the door beside it, which opened to a stairwell.

"Let's go upstairs," Mattie said, "quietly."

"I think let's stay down here. The man with the big belly said, while you went out to use the telephone, that he didn't swallow one bit of the story about how I was found by you. He said you must take them for complete fools to come in with a story like that. I know you won't get arrested, but I'll write to you in jail if you do. I know personal spelling. But I don't think we should go upstairs. I think we should just hang around here and do pretty ordinary stuff."

Mattie really wanted to go upstairs. She would bet serious money that no matter if she lived to be a hundred, she would never have another chance. There were so many things in life you only got one shot at. You'd think that knowing that, a person would take a more active part in her own life.

"Come on." She took Angelica by the hand. "One minute, I promise."

The two intruders tiptoed up the stairs. They hardly made a sound as they walked through the big door at the top.

"May I help you?" The voice coming from an open doorway hit the bare walls, ricocheting down the empty corridor. "May I help you?"

Oh, how I wish, Mattie thought, how I fervently, religiously wish that there were someone sitting in an upstairs office in the state police barracks on the Pennsylvania Turnpike, at mile marker 217, whose function in life it might be not just to offer but to deliver: help.

Not self-help, not therapy or counseling or well-crafted, smart advice. But help. The real thing. First aid. Primary assistance. A person who could take your life in hand and turn it upside down, if needed—it almost certainly would be needed—and set the whole thing right. This is not the stuff of miracles and well-intentioned angels. It would take a surer hand than that, to reorder history, rearrange all time and space. Just the restoration work on Mattie and her mother would require going back several generations, restocking the gene pool, fine tuning brain waves and temperaments and dispositions, crafting any number of new mothers worthy of the name.

A job for God. And even He inspired Saint Paul to write, "Work out your own salvation," not neglecting to add, "with fear and trembling."

"May I help you?" The voice became flesh, which followed its sounded echoes out into the hallway in the form of a little woman, not five feet tall, with Coke-bottle-bottom glasses balanced on a tiny nose. Her head was tilted to one side in a way that made her look gnomelike or maybe just more interested than usual.

If the voice asking the question had belonged to a tall, well-dressed, and polished blonde, Mattie would have responded with a smartass, "Sorry, we seem to have lost our docent. We got so caught up in the subtle play of light and shadow on the cheekbones of the police commissioner's portrait hanging in the downstairs hall." Or, if the woman had been only sturdy, ordinary, and officious, Mattie would have mumbled several convoluted things about out-of-order Coke machines and the broken toilets in the ladies' room downstairs.

As it was, Mattie said, "I'm sorry. I know we're not supposed to be up here, or even in the building. It's been two days, in fact, since I've been within one hundred miles of anywhere I'm supposed to be."

"No." The elf-woman shook her head. "You shouldn't feel that way. You're where you're meant to be. We're all of us exactly where we're meant to be. Come on in for a minute. Sit down with me. Are you two hungry at all? I have pears here and coffee cake."

"Oh no," Mattie said. "Thanks, but we can't."

Angelica gave Mattie's hand a bony-fingered, quick, mean squeeze.

"I mean," Mattie said, "maybe just for a minute. We're waiting for this little girl's mother to come pick her up."

"Oh. My," the tiny woman said. "Now wouldn't it be something, if we were all just doing that. Just waiting for our mothers to come get us, to take us home for supper and give us all our baths and our shampoos and tuck us in and read our story about animals who talk and have the usual problems with arithmetic and making paper Valentines."

And as the words were spoken, Mattie began to cry. Soft tears she couldn't stop, not even if she wanted to.

Angelica had opened up her drawing tablet and was sketching in a princess with thick glasses and a crooked neck. Mattie, standing behind the little girl, rubbed the hot tears into her cheeks, and made a complicated motion with her hand above Angelica's head and pointed to the door. The small woman nodded as though she understood, and Mattie stepped out into the corridor.

She pressed the full length of her back and legs hard up against the wall, as if to flatten her full self out straight. And Mattie cried. Her eyes scrunched tight, she moved her hand palm up, then both hands, palms raised at her side.

"Mummum mumma mummum mummum mumma mummum." The murmer came as breath, as breathing air. "I want my mumma, mummum, take me home."

And Mattie felt a warm hand take her own.

"It's all right. It's okay."

The woman held on to Mattie's hand like she was keeping her from falling off a narrow ledge five stories off the ground, and Mattie cried for hours and for days and nights, and still the small, warm hand held on.

"I'm okay," Mattie said, at last. "I'm okay."

"I know," the woman said. "I know you are."

"Oh. Angelica," Mattie said. "Angelica."

"She's fine. She's inside drawing. I closed the door. She's fine."

"Oh, you're so good to us." Mattie's legs felt long and wobbly and her arms, bony and strange. She let herself slide slowly against the wall until she rested on the smooth, cold tile floor. She could put her head down here and go to sleep.

"Are you just weary?" Angelica had opened up the door and stuck her head around the corner.

"Yes," Mattie said. "I am. I'm weary to my bones."

"Well, good," Angelica said. "I thought maybe you fell down and broke your leg or your ankle and your foot."

"Nope," Mattie said. "I didn't break a thing."

At that the large metal door swung open and a fat policeman barged in like he imagined he might be welcome.

"What in the sam hill is going on here?" He used his riot-control voice. "Madge, have you got them reports for the boss done yet? Who are these people? What are they doing up here? You need to leave here, right away. Madge, snap to."

It occurred to Mattie she should take this woman, Madge, away. Take her out and put her in the car and drive her someplace nice, a park, with a stream and tall pine trees and benches and a swing set with large, flat board seats the three of them could swing on till their toe tips touched the sky. But you can never take people with you.

"You go now," Madge said. "Everything will be okay."

"Good-bye." Angelica put a piece of folded drawing paper into Madge's hand. A princess, no doubt, a one-of-a-kind, original royal portrait. Mattie wished she had something she could give.

"Well." Mattie wanted to say something like, I'll write to you, or call you, or I'll come to visit sometime. She didn't want to say, Good-bye, I'll never see you or hear of you again in my whole life. Not one time, ever. This is it. Good-bye for good.

You can't say that to a person. You can't, Mattie thought, I don't care if they're dying. I don't care if they're dead. You cannot say those words.

"Let's move it, girls," the policeman said.

"Well, we'll see you." Mattie put her arm around Madge's skinny shoulder. "Thank you so much."

"What the fat is going on here?" the policeman was determined not to be left out.

"We'll see you," Mattie said.

"We'll see you," Madge called after them as Angelica and Mattie walked out through the open doorway and down the stairs.

The policeman pointed them in the direction of the front lobby and then made a production of standing there to watch them walk away.

"That woman was amazing," Mattie said. "She was so kind to me."

"Madge," Angelica said. "Her name is Madge."

"It's so strange," Mattie said. "It only takes about five minutes to tell if somebody's a nice person or not. Sometimes less than that. Even if a mean person tries to fake it, you can tell. Always remember that." Mattie was always giving her two sons these valuable little words to live by, instructing them to memorize and file away each one. (They had been known to use them in their own defense and Mattie's prosecution for every sort of quotidian offense: "There is never justification for raising your voice." "It doesn't cost you anything to be kind." "Try to see the other person's side.")

Angelica and Mattie went to sit in the dreary waiting area

near the woman who had welcomed them when they first came in. A young policeman was speaking to their hostess with some animation.

"Geez, what next?" he said. "That was a buddy of mine on the phone, works over at the sheriff's in Morristown. A lady comes in there with a shotgun and starts screaming she wants her kid back that they got in custody. Boys, it takes all kinds. She was ready to shoot up the place."

Ah, now there is mother love in action. Greater love hath no woman but that she arm herself with explosive firearms and storm the barricade demanding her child be returned to her.

"So what happened?" the desk monitor asked.

"Nothing." The young policeman seemed to have exhausted his supply of interest. "She fired the gun twice, hit the wall, the recoil threw her off balance, and they've got her locked up over there."

Bangs and Whimpers, Mattie thought. The whole shooting match, all of family life, is bangs and whimpers. All the pyrotechnics with no conflagration, all the pathos with no plot—no story line—all the cheap dramatics. The episode the young policeman had described epitomized what Mattie had grown up with: tears, and noise, and threats or imaginings of violence, which would come to nothing in the end. Drama, maudlin scenes, and conjured crises that all fizzled out to nothing, left you wondering what all the excitement had been about, left you bored but enervated too, too spent to think of something useful you might do, and so you organized whatever you had started lately to collect, or read, or watched TV, and waited for the next time. Mattie was forty-four, and still felt that she had yet to turn one entire day to good account, that still some measure of her time and energy were given over daily to this worried waiting, learned so early at her mother's knee. The same mother she had prayed to, cried to, not ten minutes ago, in the upstairs hallway while Madge held her hand.

She looked down at Angelica's sketch pad: a princess with an automatic rifle.

"Draw me a picture of Madge," Mattie said. "If it isn't too much trouble."

A person will always want a souvenir.

CHAPTER FOURTEEN

MATTIE WANTED A hot meal. A meal with mashed potatoes and pot roast and gravy and new peas, with pecan
pie or apple, or maybe a small slice of each, with vanilla ice
cream, to finish. The kind of meal she fancied every night at
five o'clock the whole way through both pregnancies. Home
food. She was on her way now to a diner "just down the road
a piece" from the state police barracks, or so the computer
woman said.

After a long wait under the overzealous, none-too-subtle
surveillance of three different armed policemen, Angelica's
mother had at last appeared. She had held Angelica and cried,
while the little girl patted her mother's head. We have watered
this place with our tears today, Mattie thought, baptized the
barracks with our mother sorrow.

Mattie wanted mashed potatoes. She would even settle for turkey for the rest, with walnut and apple stuffing, and orange cranberry sauce. Food her mother made. Food she still liked. So there. So what.

Mattie burrowed more deeply down into her seat. The whole scene at the police barracks made Mattie think if she survived this afternoon, this just might be her last trip to Pennsylvania. Angelica's mother had at first approached her as a kidnapper, and only Angelica had been able to convince her otherwise, saving Mattie the trouble of pointing out that it might not be state-of-the-art mothering to send your child out to public parking lots to wander into strangers' cars. Anyway, every mother should be allotted a certain quota of mistakes. Or had the mistake been Angelica's? No matter. Everybody knows a mother is responsible for everything her children do for the first twenty years of life. And if she's at all obvious about the twenty-four-hour-a-day, dogged vigilance that takes, people start slinging words at her like: interfering, controlling, overprotective, and needs-to-get-a-life.

Mattie looked at the car in front of her, Angelica and her mother, Susan. Mattie shared with them a single destination, this diner, only through a fluke, their meeting no more than a whim of time, the invention of one timepiece or another. People get thrown together into every sort of situation by no force greater than the jerky, nervous minute hand on the clock. Ninety-nine percent of whom you see, what happens in your lifetime, depends on *when* you show up where.

You take time for a second cup of coffee, you stop at the dry cleaner's *before* instead of *after*, you stop for a yellow light, for once in your life patient for the red, and time—five minutes or five seconds, one way or the other—means you're absent or you're present at the intersection of Amity Street and Lincoln Avenue when the cement truck's brakes fail; you're nowhere near, or you're right on the spot, ready to be met in a three-car collision on the James Street bridge, your split-second timing perfect for the crunch which does four hundred dollars' damage to your fender and eleven thousand dollars' damage to your neck, whose twinges will remind you for years afterward of those two and a half seconds in particular. So much that happens to you depends entirely upon time. Forget talent and good breeding and a twenty-two-inch waist. The whole thing's timing. Think about all the things in life you may have missed because you ran back into the house for an umbrella, or because you decided to let that one phone call go. Right. Think about it, Mattie, but some other time.

Mattie pulled into the parking lot under a huge sign that said THE DINER—as though there might be only one—and waved to Angelica for the tenth time since they had left the state police barracks.

Susan Perkins, Angelica's mom, had been clearly miffed when Angelica asked if she could ride to lunch in Mattie's car. Seems she had in mind some tearful reunion with her lost offspring, the sort of thing any mother might expect after a brush with total separation; that is, a show of gratitude and love of other than the usual magnitude, effusive and fairly specific thanks for the gift of life, for starters, and then for better-than-ordinary care and feeding for the upwards of twenty-five hundred days after that. But gratitude would feel an odd requirement to a child. Verbal appreciation of parental love children seldom carry to excess. Just this week Mattie had been in the car with Andy when they saw the mayor's young son holding a campaign poster for his mother's reelection.

"Would you vote for me if I were running for mayor?" Mattie had asked her son.

"That would depend," Andy said, "on who was running against you."

Angelica ran over to Mattie's car as she got out.

"I was just wondering"—Angelica took Mattie's hand—"if you were still wanting to buy me ice cream, since you never got a chance."

"Sure," Mattie said.

Angelica called out to her mother, "Mom, can we let her buy me an ice cream since she's been wanting to for about six hours?"

Once inside, Angelica ordered an English muffin and a banana split; Mattie decided to get the pork roast dinner with mashed potatoes and gravy and three vegetables—as long as someone had gone to all the trouble of making it—and Susan got the fruit and cottage cheese dieter's special, with a double order of fries.

"So what brings you to Pennsylvania?" Susan lighted a long, pencil-skinny cigarette. "Not enough action for you in Massachusetts?"

Susan had been downright hostile in their first exchange, but she seemed to have gotten it out of her system. Her tone was easy.

"I grew up here," Mattie said, "and my mother died here."

"When you were growing up?"

"No, today. I mean yesterday. I'm sort of out of it. I've been driving for two days."

"From Massachusetts?"

"Yeah. I got a little sidetracked." Mattie helped the waitress slide four tiny dishes into a small circle around her dinner plate. "I picked up two women, three really, no four, along the way, but it's not a very interesting story."

"I'll take your word for it." Susan gave a long exhale and the smoke thinned crossing Angelica's banana split, disappearing at the wall behind Angelica. "I'm sorry about your mother," Susan said. "Were you close?"

"No, not close, not the good way. I think I hung on to the idea of her with something of a stranglehold though. Or the idea of her hung on to me that way."

It seemed to Mattie that ever since her mother's death she had been giving everyone these intense, psychologically truthful answers, if they so much as said hello.

"What's stranglehold?" Angelica had chocolate syrup on both cheeks and her chin. Her English muffin sat undisturbed.

"Strangle," Susan said and reached across the table circling Angelica's neck with both hands and making ghoulish sounds.

Angelica giggled. "That's what I thought," she said and began moving peanuts and pieces of pineapple to a pile on top of one banana. "I only like certain ingredients," Angelica said.

"I used to get banana splits when I was little," Mattie said. "In the drugstore. You broke a balloon and there was a number inside to say how much you paid, from one cent to thirty-nine cents. I usually got a thirty-four or thirty-five."

"They still do that with balloons at the Big Bopper at my town," Angelica said.

"Yeah, but it's not really the same," Mattie said. "Nothing's the same as it was. Like there was all this good stuff that's gone, but I also feel like my life was awful growing up with my mother."

"One of these abusers?" Susan said.

"Oh, no, nothing like that. I don't think she even really noticed me much."

"What are 'busers?'" Angelica said.

"People who knock you over and play mean and are generally no fun to have around," Susan said.

"Oh."

"My mother would never have defined *abuse* or *stranglehold* for me. She never told me anything. I asked her in sixth grade what queers were and she said they were people who were bad. I thought she meant they stole things from the five-and-ten."

"No wonder you weren't close." Susan lighted another cigarette. The french fry plate was empty, but the mound of cottage cheese appeared to be in its original condition.

"I don't expect you to understand this," Mattie said, "but all along I've always felt so cut off, and now she dies and I feel like maybe I never separated from her at all, now that she's not around to separate from anymore."

"I had a shrink once who said the best way to separate from your parents was to get more intimate with them, open up to them completely, let them get to know you and get to know them, too. He said that was the only way he knew to separate. It worked for him. He used to tell me a lot about his grief with his mother. There was a real doozie, if you ever want to know one."

"Doozie. I haven't heard that for years. Not since Pennsylvania."

"This is Pennsylvania," Susan said.

"Oh, right. I keep thinking I'm nowhere. Get intimate, you say. It sounds right. It really does sound right, but how are you supposed to get intimate with a potato, get intimate with a ball bearing."

"That bad, huh," Susan said.

"What's a ball bearing?" Angelica's banana split had

decomposed. The dish held almost as much as when she started but in a grossly altered form.

"No idea," Susan said. "Ball bearing is one of those words adults use and they all know what they mean, but you ask them to define it and they say it's a metal thing, or they tell you to go look it up."

"Besides," Mattie said, "that advice isn't too handy when your mother's dead."

"Look," Susan said, "I'm just telling you what my shrink said he did. I don't even think he was suggesting I try it. In fact, I'm sure he wasn't. He told me if he had my parents, he'd move to another state and change his name."

"What's wrong with your parents?" Mattie said.

"Alcohol. Bloody Marys for breakfast, martinis for lunch—four martinis, if you're counting—and then the serious drinking starts in the late afternoon."

"Gee, I'm sorry."

"Yeah, well."

"See, that's always how it is," Mattie said. "I hear about other people's mothers and I think I should feel lucky; only I don't. I never do. A lot of people seem to just do okay in spite of anything. Like you."

"Hey, look, anybody can seem put together at lunch—especially if we order dessert."

"No, I mean it," Mattie said. "You seem resilient and like you know what you're about, as though your mother didn't cripple you like mine did me."

"It's a nice excuse if you can find a buyer." Susan's words were followed by another long, smoky exhale.

"You're predisposing your child to lung cancer, you

know," Mattie said, "not to mention what you're doing to your own lungs."

Susan raised an eyebrow.

"See, I'm being obnoxious," Mattie said. "Most of the people I happen to like best in the world are smokers, but I always do that. It's like when there's a dry spot in the conversation, I insult somebody."

"And that's your mother's fault, too." Susan blew a thin thread of smoke away from Mattie.

"Well, I guess I always thought it was," Mattie said. "Either that or I'm the bad one, and if it's me then I guess it means I'm just plain awful, really evil inside."

"This is turning into one of those conversations one person should be paying the other person money for."

"Sorry, I've been very needy ever since yesterday."

"Hey," Susan said. "A person losing her mother, it's a real big thing."

CHAPTER FIFTEEN

MATTIE ROLLED THE window down and tried to think of something new to do. There were a limited number of alternatives when you were driving and alone, and usually you got to all of them before lunch the first day. Mattie had hardly spoken to Angelica in the restaurant, and then they said good-bye, not pretending they would meet again. Over and done with. Just like that.

And then there was Angelica's mother, Susan. About twenty-seven years old and a chain-smoker to boot.

Motherhood. Mattie clicked her teeth together loudly. Maybe the whole problem was motherhood, a concept over-loaded, flawed and doomed from its inception, an arrangement far too complicated for the average person. The book of Genesis wrote it up as one of those off-the-cuff decisions devised as the curse rolls off the tongue. An edict born of anger. "Get out of Eden, and take the woman with you. By the sweat of your brow. . . . From this day forward. . ." That part was reasonable enough when the alternative was puttering around the garden, a few rounds of golf, and every hole with Eve, and conversation every afternoon, again with Eve. How much do you have to say to each other in the evening when you haven't been a moment out of one another's company all day? No, the sweat-of-your-brow part seemed fine; it was the motherhood arrangement that let you know you'd left the garden of Eden for good.

For nine months, two hundred and eighty days for textbook cases, you carry someone in your body: flesh of your flesh, bone of your bone, born, you'll think, entirely of your spirit by the time you've pushed him out, and found out in the first eleven minutes of his life that you have been operating on only partial information up until that moment. Then before the stitches heal, the separating starts. Or call it losing. Eve only got the word on labor pains, but that was the good news.

It was the business of mothering, year after year, where you got into heavy waters. If it had been set up so that you worked toward perfection, that would have been a reasonable arrangement, diapers, colic, college, notwithstanding. But you start out with perfection and you learn to give it up, to live without, and that's full vindication for a dozen lifetimes of three-times-a-day consumption of whole bushel baskets of forbidden fruit. Let the punishment fit the crime. Wasn't that also in the book of Genesis, or maybe that was Gilbert and Sullivan. Either way. Giving up your child, as mothers are required to do, is way out of line, no matter how you figure it.

Mattie had never classified her own being a mother with

her mother's being a mother, never had allowed that they might be the same in any way. She and her mother had been involved in different enterprises altogether: Mattie's mother fell short, missed the mark, messed up, completely blew it; Mattie herself did the best she could. That kind of not-the-same-in-any-way.

And so, now what? Her mother dies, and all of a sudden motherhood is motherhood. She dies, and the next afternoon it turns out she and Mattie were engaged in the same undertaking all along. And open up the drawstring wide and throw in Bea and Babette, herself a mother (God, please pay particular attention), and toss in the mothers of Angelica and Sherry Hicks and Sherry's own newborn. Sherry as a mother. Mothers every one. And then damn them, or forgive them all. One trial for the species. No individual culpability. We have an institution here found to be seriously defective. The gavel crashes down and judgment is pronounced:

"Here ye. Here ye. All attend. Be it hereafter fully and completely comprehended that motherhood is not a workable arrangement." Case closed.

Or send recommendations back to a committee, made up entirely of the sons and daughters of mothers, sons and daughters who still have mothers of their own, alive and well in Brooklyn or Miami or in Arkansas, or in their heads, mothers whom they might consult by mail, or telephone, or in their own off-the-cuff responses when they're tired.

And every mother that you call upon—alive or dead—will have a different answer. Pregnant Sherry's mother, fresh from a reunion of relations, will provide an answer with her version of mother love spelled out in explicatives and vituperation. Sherry, caught between contractions, will suggest no one should give birth in the first place. Bea will tell you, Go with it, however it turns out, and make a good case for the laundry and the housework of the thing, and sit then staring out the window at the passing scenery, not dissatisfied. Ask Babette and watch her shrug and say What do you mean? and freshen up her lipstick. Don't bother asking Jeannie. Angelica's mother, Susan, will be impatient with the question, and behave as though the answer were too obvious to say.

So, Mattie thought. Is this it then? A general amnesty proclaimed out on Route 80, swarms of mothers pouring out from behind trees and bushes on the highway, coming out, hands held high overhead. "I didn't do it." "I did it but I didn't mean to." "It was only what was done to me." Ten thousand aprons wrung in unison, and nary an interesting excuse. What else can you do? Put every mother in America in jail.

Mattie shifted her weight. Not the solidest of rock foundations for a resolution.

And it's only half of the conundrum anyway, and certain not to be the toughest part. If you throw a blanket, a worn patchwork quilt, over the whole institution of motherhood, and say, "Nobody's perfect," or something equally forgiving, you're still left with how to negotiate the remainder of the afternoon, and the whole day that will come after that. You'll have to puzzle out just how you intend to go about picking up your own life and running with it.

The mother must give up the child she bears; but the child must give up the mother, too. Try that one on for size, Mattie thought. She clung beyond all reason, wed to hating, held in the clutches of remembering every miss along the way.

Mattie felt estranged and entangled all at the same time. At her most relaxed she heard her mother speak when she spoke, saw her move and gesture with the same intent, identical effect. Mattie worried that she and her mother were the same in deep core ways. That they shared not just the same chin and hairline but the same symptoms, the same spirit, the same soul.

Mother, now as then, my shield and my staff, my sustenance. The woman responsible for the steel that is my spine, for my resolve, my showing up late, but my arrival after all. My fortitude, my shield—did I say that?—my shield and buckler, fire by night and cloud by day. With any other cushion I might have sunk in and never surfaced. You woman—springboard and departure ticket, after all. You made it so easy for me to leave, to walk away. We both know what a sorry pillar of salt I would have been, straining, chafing, standing there.

"You let me go," Mattie said out loud.

You gave me no other choice. There was nothing to stay for.

Freedom—not a mean gift, shield and buckler. You let go perfectly, I think, but I intend to be too tired to ever know for sure, strength and shield, steel sustenance, sustainer of my flesh, you must have been, at least at first, before the cans of Campbell's Scotch Broth soup I opened by myself and added water to, warmed up, and ate alone when I was just thirteen. "I cannot cook for you for your whole life," you said, and rightly so, that day. But till that declaration you must have nourished me; I am arrived alive to meet this hour.

Shield and buckler, am I getting this thing right? I am fooled so easily, betrayed by my own misconstruction and meanderings.

And do you hear me this afternoon from the far side of the grave, when you refused to hear all I refused to say the day we sat together in the summer, each of us as skittish as the other, eager to be up and away?

CHAPTER SIXTEEN

MATTIE HAD BEEN on her way an hour, then another hour. Soon she would be close enough to stop measuring the time.

GRANBY   27 MILES

And, oh, the journey. Oh, the strange companions on the way. Mattie crowded her several female acquaintances, all met in one thousand-hour day, into an oversize family van and pointed it in the general direction of the Pacific Ocean. An outing no more random, no more fanciful, or no less reasoned-out than family life. In the years that Mattie was growing up, life at home had no more intentionality than these chance encounters on Route 80. When Mattie's parents were in the business of raising children, life had been no more planned or thought out in advance than random meetings at Joe's Bar or the State Police Barracks. Every new event, each new family member, came as some surprise. Nothing, no one, had been anticipated properly.

A family should be a planful thing, a thing, ideally, you could sit down and write a paragraph about before it happened. Even this death was such a willy-nilly thing, come out of nowhere, without foreshadowing or warning. Willy-nilly all the way, from birth to age seventy. And there was nothing to say that this life could not have been lived out some whole different way.

Mattie had a dream a few months ago. She dreamed that she was at a party, a fancy-dress affair with men in ties and tails and women all in evening gowns, and across the crowded room Mattie had seen her mother, only in the dream she was a little girl, maybe six or seven, standing with her back to Mattie, wearing a skimpy, thin cotton dresss, her skinny arms and legs too long, her little shoulders hunched. Then she turned and spotted Mattie and she changed; she smiled and winked and made a silly face and stooped in an elaborate curtsy, then took a glass of punch and walked so carefully over to a big chair and sat down, poised and really lovely, and Mattie could see her dress was actually a light blue watered silk. She raised her cup to Mattie in a toast and drank, a little girl delighted to be at the party, even all by herself, and anyone could see, she was a child whose life might turn out a hundred different ways.

Mattie lowered the sun visor. Driving west to Granby, the light always tried to blind you at some stage of the journey. Mattie groped in her handbag until she found her sunglasses and put them on. The effect was wonderful. The brown hills in the distance took on an auburn cast, every color of the changing sky looked rich and certain, the pointy little evergreens dotting the median turned a true forest green. Mattie thought she should wear sunglasses all the time. Just adding on a little bit of color could make the world look very nice.

On one visit home to Granby, all the relatives had gone over to Nancy's house for a cookout. Mattie always felt like she was there on sufferance and might be asked to leave at any point, and so was keeping a low profile—well, low for her. Mattie took a rounded spoonful of baked beans and one of coleslaw, one of potato salad, one of bright red Jell-o with apples and banana slices and miniature marshmallow bits, and she drank a great deal of Nehi orange crush, enough to go home feeling slightly sick. She said no-thank-you to the sloppy joes and to the bakery birthday cake. In a family, it is almost always someone's birthday, or close enough.

Nancy spoke to Mattie that night for the first time just as the aunts, who were always the first to leave, began shuffling around, collecting plates and pans they'd brought their contributions in, saying, "Why not" to offers of leftover pie and salads, saying over and again, "Now where did that pocketbook take off to?"

"Are you familiar with the painter of true light?" Nancy had said to Mattie that night.

Mattie called to mind her friend Tom, a painter, who did things with light and shadow that could soothe her soul. She had a print of one of his paintings in her kitchen, one in which the light of the late afternoon is broken up by mullioned windowpanes: the tiny blocks of faded light lay out across the floor and creep up walls and onto furniture.

"Come see this painting that I bought." Nancy had spoken softly, for the moment oblivious of the aunts' confusion. "I have three of them."

And Mattie had followed her into the front room where Nancy pointed to a mostly pink and sky-blue pastel painting of a fussy house surrounded by too many flowers and far too much sky. A trite brook ran beneath a little arching bridge, made of the same white spindles that held up the railing on the porch. Mattie wanted to make fun of it—at least inside her head—to memorize each pretty dab of paint, to reuse when she told her friends how different she was from her sister. Only she couldn't. You can't make fun of sadness, and you can't memorize it either. You don't want to.

The painting had all the aesthetic appeal of a giftshop display of those ceramic Victorian shops and houses, each with a small light bulb burning inside to shine out of all the tiny windows. The painting took up most of one whole wall.

Nancy had moved to the dimmer switch on the far wall and turned it slowly back and forth.

"See, it depends on how bright your room is, how you see it. Whether you see the light coming from the sky and the sunset, with the evening falling all around outside the empty house, or whether you see that the sky's already dark, and yellow lights are shining out from all the windows."

Nancy kept working the dimmer switch very slowly dark to light. "Sometimes," she said, "sometimes it just depends upon the weather, what you see. Sometimes just the time of day, the angle of the light that's coming in, can make all the difference."

You can be somebody's sister forty years, and she can still surprise you.

The road ahead of Mattie was suddenly lit up with red lights. Mattie hit the brakes, slowing to a full stop like everybody else. In the distance she could see a snake-line of cars stretched out as far as the horizon. Mattie turned the car off, put her head back, closed her eyes.

"Wake me when it's time for dinner." Mattie sat perfectly

still for several minutes, then leaned forward, blinked, and looked around. Up ahead, people had gotten out to mill around, to ask and tell each other what they thought was going on. Mattie opened the car door and sat not thinking, then got out and started to walk. She would be very careful not to speak to anyone, and if perchance someone were to ask her for a lift to any U.S. airport or look the least bit pregnant, she would yawn and amble back toward the car, making sure to check the backseat and the trunk compartment before she drove off down the middle of the field.

Mattie moved along the never-ending line of cars she could imagine stretching all the way to the West Coast, the front car in the line perched precariously at land's end, rocking back and forth a bit. The people who stood about in clumps, or all alone, gave little evidence of impatience, ambling here and there or chatting; some stood studying a map or the mountains in the distance as though they would have had to stop at this point anyway to reconsider things, to have a look around, and maybe think about a whole new destination.

Mattie felt like the observer, the one who came to watch, while everybody else was caught up some way in the action. Mattie walked on, stomped on, covering some distance. If traffic started up again, she would have a real race to get back to her car. But no one was going anywhere. That was obvious. Everyone was stuck, stranded on the way. Mattie walked faster. She was good at walking fast, always a half-step in front of whomever she walked with. It drove both of her husbands crazy. No one else had ever mentioned it. She let her arms swing freely, feeling limber, easy.

Up ahead, Mattie finally saw the cause for the delay. A tractor trailer truck lay on its side across the two lanes of highway with a straight cut down one side, and all around it, covering the asphalt and grassy shoulder, down the incline into the ravine were bright blue boxes of detergent. Cheer. With red and white and yellow dots of color on the boxes everywhere. Thousands—maybe millions—no, probably thousands of boxes of soap powder. Mattie looked around at other faces, ready to smile at them and shake her head just slightly, side to side, and look pleased, and amazed, and disapproving, all at the same time. But she caught no one's eye. They had all been standing here for ten or fifteen minutes, long enough to have gotten over some large measure of the wonder, long enough almost to be used to it, and to be thinking about where they would be going after this, and just when that might be.

Mattie crossed over to the far side of the roadway and climbed up the steep little grade, and sat down, tucking her skirts around her legs like Bermuda shorts. She propped her legs up, cupped her chin in both hands, and started humming, "Oh, I wish I were an apple a' hangin' on a tree and everyone who came along…" interwoven with snatches of another song she couldn't put words to.

A man who had to be the driver stood smoking by the truck, looking important and busy, even standing there alone. He was obviously unharmed. It gave you such a good feeling, like at the end of a movie starring Gene Hackman where the underdogs win in the last few minutes. It made you feel that things usually do turn out okay: the truck does a double flip, spilling its guts across the roadway, and the driver walks away, or gets into another truck, lights up a cigarette, and drives off to Oregon.

Four or five police cars stood parked at odd uncalculated angles, with their lights blinking, their drivers and their passengers talking to one another, casual, but obviously waiting.

Mattie thought they might organize the crowd to pile the boxes of Cheer in towers by the side of the road, or toss them all, at least for the time being, in one direction, out of the way. But anyone could tell the job was too big, bigger even than the crowd. It was so big that you could only sit and watch it there, and talk about how no cars, not even one, had been involved in the crash, how lucky it was really, and to say what it reminded you of.

The air here was so clean and clear. It was as though you could see straight through it. The people down below moved randomly, and in slow motion, or in slower motion than when they were doing something that had been their own idea in the first place. They looked like actors on a set taking five, milling here and there; the set so cleverly designed as to seem wide open, limitless, stretching out as far as the imagination. And Mattie had the best seat in the house.

She wished a teenager would happen by, hefting a twenty-four-pound boom box, playing "Groovy Kind of Love," the version from 1964 or the newer one, it wouldn't matter. Or that a small chamber orchestra would separate themselves out singly from the ragtag collection down below, and that a few middle-aged moving men dressed in gray, or dull gray-blue, would hustle in with chairs and metal music stands, and the musicians would sit down, smoothing the floor-length skirts of their black rayon dresses which look better from a distance; adjusting ties and tails, and tune up like they had from now until tomorrow afternoon if that was what was needed, and would play Canon in D by Pachelbel to get things rolling, then a little Mozart, and whatever would seem right to them just after that.

And a wooden wagon drawn by one old horse with a

laconic disposition would move slowly, bump along across the middle of the median, and stop at some spot that made sense to him, and two buxom women, but with faces you could tell were flushed and pink and pretty at a still remembered seventeen, two buxom women on whose breasts the heads of children lay, back then and still sometimes today, would pour from pitchers frosted, dripping cold, a lemonade the color of the yellow aprons that they wore.

And then, just after dark, the dancing would begin. At first, only children dancing, a few with mothers, smiling, limber, lithe, light on their feet. Then couples who were obviously in love, then older people, slower and more settled, but surprising in the way that they could move. Then everyone, under the moon and the pink and blue and yellow Japanese lanterns, and you would see long tables piled with food, just at the moment when you realized you were hungry.

Mattie stood up, brushed herself off. It really was time to be on her way. Traffic would start moving soon now, would pass by single file, in a trickle, and Mattie, like everybody else in turn, would slow down, take one more look, as she drove by. Then home, a straight shot, not far now, even with delays, and Paul and the boys would be there before dark.